BOOKS BY
ALEXANDER McCALL SMITH

IN THE NO. 1 LADIES' DETECTIVE AGENCY SERIES

The No. 1 Ladies' Detective Agency
Tears of the Giraffe
Morality for Beautiful Girls
The Kalahari Typing School for Men
The Full Cupboard of Life
In the Company of Cheerful Ladies
Blue Shoes and Happiness
The Good Husband of Zebra Drive
The Miracle at Speedy Motors
Tea Time for the Traditionally Built
The Double Comfort Safari Club

IN THE ISABEL DALHOUSIE SERIES

The Sunday Philosophy Club
Friends, Lovers, Chocolate
The Right Attitude to Rain
The Careful Use of Compliments
The Comforts of a Muddy Saturday
The Lost Art of Gratitude

IN THE PORTUGUESE IRREGULAR VERBS SERIES

Portuguese Irregular Verbs
The Finer Points of Sausage Dogs
At the Villa of Reduced Circumstances

IN THE 44 SCOTLAND STREET SERIES

44 Scotland Street
Espresso Tales
Love over Scotland
The World According to Bertie
The Unbearable Lightness of Scones

The Girl Who Married a Lion and Other Tales from Africa
La's Orchestra Saves the World

THE DOUBLE COMFORT SAFARI CLUB

THE DOUBLE COMFORT

SAFARI CLUB

Alexander McCall Smith

Pantheon Books

New York

All rights reserved. Published in the United States by Pantheon Books, a division of Random House, Inc., New York. Originally published in Great Britain by Little, Brown, an imprint of Little, Brown Book Group, London.

Pantheon Books and colophon are registered trademarks of Random House, Inc.

ISBN 978-1-61129-064-6

Printed in the United States of America

This book is for Anne Marie McLaughlin,
a friend of Mma Ramotswe,
and of those in need

THE DOUBLE COMFORT SAFARI CLUB

CHAPTER ONE

YOU DO NOT CHANGE PEOPLE
BY SHOUTING AT THEM

NO CAR, thought Mr. J.L.B. Matekoni, that great mechanic, and good man. *No car . . .*

He paused. It was necessary, he felt, to order the mind when one was about to think something profound. And Mr. J.L.B. Matekoni was at that moment on the verge of an exceptionally important thought, even though its final shape had yet to reveal itself. How much easier it was for Mma Ramotswe—she put things so well, so succinctly, so profoundly, and appeared to do this with such little effort. It was very different if one was a mechanic, and therefore not used to telling people—in the nicest possible way, of course—how to run their lives. Then one had to think quite hard to find just the right words that would make people sit up and say, "But that is very true, Rra!" Or, especially if you were Mma Ramotswe, "But surely that is well known!"

He had very few criticisms to make of Precious Ramotswe, his wife and founder of the No. 1 Ladies' Detective Agency, but *if* one were to make a list of her faults—which would be a minuscule document, barely visible, indeed, to the naked eye—one would perhaps have to include a tendency (only a slight tendency, of course) to claim that things that she happened to believe were *well known*. This phrase gave these beliefs a sort of unassailable authority, the status that went with facts that all right-thinking people would readily acknowledge—such as the fact that the sun rose in the east, over the undulating canopy of acacia that stretched along Botswana's border, over the waters of the great Limpopo River itself that now, at the height of the rainy season, flowed deep and fast towards the ocean half a continent away. Or the fact that Seretse Khama had been the first President of Botswana; or even the truism that Botswana was one of the finest and most peaceful countries in the world. All of these facts were indeed both incontestable and well known; whereas Mma Ramotswe's pronouncements, to which she attributed the special status of being well known, were often, rather, statements of opinion. There was a difference, thought Mr. J.L.B. Matekoni, but it was not one he was planning to point out; there were some things, after all, that it was not *helpful* for a husband to say to his wife, and that, he thought, was probably one of them.

Now, his thoughts having been properly marshalled, the right words came to him in a neat, economical expression: *No car is entirely perfect.* That was what he wanted to say, and these words were all that was needed to say it. So he said it once more. *No car is entirely perfect.*

In his experience, which was considerable—as the proprietor of Tlokweng Road Speedy Motors and attending physician, therefore, to a whole fleet of middle-ranking cars—every vehicle had its bad points, its foibles, its rattles, its complaints; and this, he thought, was the language of machinery, those idiosyncratic engine sounds by which a car would strive to communicate with those with ears to listen, usually mechanics. Every car had its good points too: a comfortable driving seat, perhaps, moulded over the years to the shape of the car's owner, or an engine that started the first time without hesitation or complaint, even on the coldest winter morning, when the air above Botswana was dry and crisp and sharp in the lungs. Each car, then, was an individual, and if only he could get his apprentices to grasp that fact, their work might be a little bit more reliable and less prone to require redoing by him. *Push, shove, twist:* these were no mantras for a good mechanic. *Listen, coax, soothe:* that should be the motto inscribed above the entrance to every garage; that, or the words which he had once seen printed on the advertisement for a garage in Francistown: *Your car is ours.*

That slogan, persuasive though it might have sounded, had given him pause. It was a little ambiguous, he decided: on the one hand, it might be taken to suggest that the garage was in the business of taking people's cars away from them—an unfortunate choice of words if read that way. On the other, it could mean that the garage staff treated clients' cars with the same care that they treated their own. That, he thought, is what they meant, and it would have been preferable if they had said it. *It is always better to say what you mean*—it was his wife, Mma Ramotswe, who said that, and he had always assumed that she meant it.

No, he mused: there is no such thing as a perfect car, and if every car had its good and bad points, it was the same with people. Just as every person had his or her little ways—habits that niggled or irritated others, annoying mannerisms, vices and failings, moments of selfishness—so too did they have their good points: a winning smile, an infectious sense of humour, the ability to cook a favourite dish just the way you wanted it.

That was the way the world was; it was composed of a few almost perfect people (ourselves); then there were a good many people who generally did their best but were not all that perfect (our friends and colleagues); and finally, there were a few rather nasty ones (our enemies and opponents). Most people fell into that middle group—those who did their best—and the last group was, thankfully, very small and not much in evidence in places like Botswana, where he was fortunate enough to live.

These reflections came to Mr. J.L.B. Matekoni while he was driving his tow-truck down the Lobatse Road. He was on what Mma Ramotswe described as one of his errands of mercy. In this case he was setting out to rescue the car of one Mma Constance Mateleke, a senior and highly regarded midwife and, as it happened, a long-standing friend of Mma Ramotswe. She had called him from the roadside. "Quite dead," said Mma Mateleke through the faint, crackling line of her mobile phone. "Stopped. Plenty of petrol. Just stopped like that, Mr. Matekoni. Dead."

Mr. J.L.B. Matekoni smiled to himself. "No car dies forever," he consoled her. "When a car *seems* to die, it is sometimes just sleeping. Like Lazarus, you know." He was not quite sure of the analogy. As a boy he had heard the story of Lazarus at Sunday school in Molepolole, but his recollection was now hazy. It was many years ago, and the stories of that time, the real, the made-up, the long-winded tales of the old people—all of these had a tendency to get mixed up and become one. There were seven lean cows in somebody's dream, or was it five lean cows and seven fat ones?

"So you are calling yourself Jesus Christ now, are you, Mr. Matekoni? No more Tlokweng Road Speedy Motors, is it? Jesus Christ Motors now?" retorted Mma Mateleke. "You say that you can raise cars from the dead. Is that what you're saying?"

Mr. J.L.B. Matekoni chuckled. "Certainly not. No, I am just a mechanic, but I know how to wake cars up. That is not a special thing. Any mechanic can wake a car." Not apprentices, though, he thought.

"We'll see," she said. "I have great faith in you, Mr. Matekoni, but this car seems very sick now. And time is running away. Perhaps we should stop talking on the phone and you should be getting into your truck to come and help me."

So it was that he came to be travelling down the Lobatse Road, on a pleasantly fresh morning, allowing his thoughts to wander on the broad subject of perfection and flaws. On either side of the road the country rolled out in a grey-green carpet of thorn bush, stretching off into the distance, to where the rocky outcrops of the hills marked the end of the land and the beginning of the sky. The rains had brought thick new grass sprouting up between the trees; this was good, as the cattle would soon become fat on the abundant sweet forage it provided. And it was good for Botswana too, as fat cattle meant fat people—not too fat, of course, but well-fed and prosperous-looking; people who were happy to be who they were and where they were.

Yes, thought Mr. J.L.B. Matekoni, even if no country was absolutely perfect, Botswana, surely, came as close as one could get. He closed his eyes in contentment, and then quickly remembered that he was driving, and opened them again. A car behind him—not a car that he recognised—had driven to within a few feet of the rear of his tow-truck, and was aggressively looking for an opportunity to pass. The problem, though, was that the Lobatse Road was busy with traffic coming the other way, and there was a vehicle in front of Mr. J.L.B. Matekoni that was in no hurry to get anywhere; it was a driver like Mma Potokwane, he imagined, who ambled along and frequently knocked the gear-stick out of gear as she waved her hand to emphasise some point she was making to a passenger. Yet Mma Potokwane, and this slow driver ahead of him, he reminded himself, had a right to take things gently if they wished. Lobatse would not go away, and whether one reached it at eleven in the morning or half past eleven would surely matter very little.

He looked in his rear-view mirror. He could not make out the face of the driver, who was sitting well back in his seat, and he could not therefore engage in eye contact with him. He should calm down, thought Mr. J.L.B. Matekoni, rather than . . . His line of thought was interrupted by the sudden swerving of the other vehicle as it pulled over sharply to the left. Mr. J.L.B. Matekoni, well versed as he was in the ways of every sort of driver, gripped his steering wheel hard and muttered under his breath. What was being attempted was that most dangerous of manoeuvres—overtaking on the wrong side.

He steered a steady course, carefully applying his brakes so as to allow the other driver ample opportunity to effect his passing as quickly as possible. Not that he deserved the consideration, of course, but Mr. J.L.B. Matekoni knew that when another driver did something dangerous it was best to allow him to finish what he was doing and get out of the way.

In a cloud of dust and gravel chips thrown up off the unpaved verge of the road, the impatient car shot past, before swerving again to get back onto the tarmac. Mr. J.L.B. Matekoni felt the urge to lean on his horn and flash his lights in anger, but he did neither of these things. The other driver knew that what he had done was wrong; there was no need to engage in an abusive exchange which would lead nowhere, and would certainly not change that driver's ways. "You do not change people by shouting at them," Mma Ramotswe had once observed. And she was right: sounding one's horn, shouting—these were much the same things, and achieved equally little.

And then an extraordinary thing happened. The impatient driver, his illegal manoeuvre over, and now clear of the tow-truck, looked in his mirror and gave a scrupulously polite thank-you wave to Mr. J.L.B. Matekoni. And Mr. J.L.B. Matekoni, taken by surprise, responded with an equally polite wave of acknowledgement, as one would reply to any roadside courtesy or show of

good driving manners. That was the curious thing about Botswana; even when people were rude—and some degree of human
rudeness was inevitable—they were rude in a fairly polite way.

The road was climbing at this point, and the other car soon
disappeared over the brow of the hill. Mr. J.L.B. Matekoni wondered why the driver had been in such a rush. He could be late
for an appointment, perhaps; or he could be a lawyer due to make
an appearance in the High Court down there. That could be awkward, of course, and might just explain a certain amount of
speeding. He had heard from a lawyer whose car he fixed that it
was a serious matter to be late in court, not only from the lawyer's
point of view, but from that of the client as well, as the judge
would hardly be sympathetic to somebody who had kept him
waiting. But even if that driver was a lawyer, and even if he was
running late, it would not excuse passing on the wrong side,
which put the lives of others in danger. Nothing excused that sort
of thing.

Mr. J.L.B. Matekoni found himself wondering what Mma
Ramotswe would have said about this. When he had first got to
know her, he had been surprised at her ability to watch the doings
of others and then come up with a completely credible explanation of their motives. Now, however, he took that for granted, and
merely nodded in agreement when she explained to him even the
most opaque acts of others. Of course that was why this or that
was done; of course that was why somebody said what they did,
or did not say it, depending on the circumstances. Mma Ramotswe simply *understood*.

He imagined himself telling her that evening: "I saw a very
bad bit of driving on the Lobatse Road this morning. Really bad."

She would nod. "Nothing new there, Mr. J.L.B. Matekoni."

"A man shot past me on the wrong side. Whoosh! He was in
a very big hurry to get to Lobatse." He would pause, and then

would come the casual query, "Why do you think somebody would risk his neck—and mine too—to get down to Lobatse so quickly?"

Mma Ramotswe would look thoughtful. "A new car?" she asked. "A big one?"

"A very big one," said Mr. J.L.B. Matekoni. "Three-point-six-litre engine with continuous variable-valve timing . . ."

"Yes, yes." Mma Ramotswe did not need these mechanical details. "And the colour of the car?"

"Red. Bright red."

Mma Ramotswe smiled. "And the driver? Did you see anything of the driver?"

"Not really. Just the back of his head. But he was a very polite bad driver. He thanked me after he had passed me on the wrong side. He actually thanked me."

Mma Ramotswe nodded. "He must be having an affair, that man. He must be rushing off to see a lady. I suspect he was late, and did not want to keep her waiting."

"Come on now, Mma! How can you tell that just from the colour of the car?"

"There is that. But there is also the politeness. He is a man who is feeling pleased with the world and grateful for something. So he thanked you."

He went over this imaginary conversation in his head. He could just hear her, and her explanation, and he thought how she would probably be right, even if he could not see how she could reach a conclusion on the basis of such slender evidence. But that was the difference between Mma Ramotswe, a detective, and him, a mere mechanic. That was a very significant difference, and . . .

He paused. On the road before him, still some way in the distance, but unmistakable, he could see a car pulled up at the side of the road, a car that he recognised as belonging to Mma Mateleke. And just beyond it, also pulled up at the side of the road, was the large red car that had shot past him a few minutes previously. The driver had got out of the red car and was standing beside Mma Mateleke's window, looking for all the world as if he had stopped to chat with an old friend encountered along the road. He had been in such a terrible rush, and yet here he was, stopping to talk. What would Mma Ramotswe make of this, Mr. J.L.B. Matekoni wondered, as he began to apply the brakes of his truck.

Mma Mateleke had got out of her car by the time Mr. J.L.B. Matekoni had parked safely on the verge. She greeted him warmly as he approached.

"Well, well, I am a very lucky lady today," she said. "Here you are, Mr. Matekoni, with that truck of yours. And here is another man, too, who happened to be passing. It is very nice for a lady in distress to have two strong men at her side."

As she spoke she looked in the direction of the driver of the red car. He smiled, acknowledging the compliment, and then turned to Mr. J.L.B. Matekoni.

"This is Mr. Ntirang," said Mma Mateleke. "He was travelling down to Lobatse and he saw me by the side of the road."

Mr. Ntirang nodded gravely, as if to confirm a long and complicated story. "Her car had clearly broken down," he said to Mr. J.L.B. Matekoni. "And this is miles from anywhere." He paused before adding, "As you can see."

Mr. J.L.B. Matekoni took a piece of cloth from his pocket and wiped his hands. It was a habit he had, as a mechanic, stemming from the days when he had used lint in the garage and was always removing grease. Now it had become a nervous gesture, almost, like straightening one's cuffs or wiping one's brow.

"Yes," he said, meeting the other man's gaze. "This is far from everywhere, although . . ." He hesitated. He did not want to be rude, but he could not let the bad driving he had witnessed go unremarked upon. "Although this is a busy road, isn't it? And quite a dangerous one, too, with all the bad driving one sees."

There was silence, but only a brief one. There was birdsong, from an acacia tree behind the fence that ran along the edge of the road; the sound of the bush. There was always birdsong.

Mr. Ntirang did not drop his eyes when he spoke, nor did he look away. "Oh, yes, Rra. Bad driving! There are some very bad drivers around. People who cannot drive straight. People who go from one side of the road to the other. People who drink *while* they drive—not driving after you've been drinking, but driving *while* you're drinking. There are all of these things." He turned to Mma Mateleke. "Aren't there, Mma?"

Mma Mateleke glanced at her watch. She did not seem particularly interested in this conversation. "Maybe," she said. "There are many instances of bad behaviour, but I do not think that we have time to talk about them right now." She turned to Mr. J.L.B. Matekoni. "Could you take a look, Rra, and see what is wrong with this car of mine?"

Mr. J.L.B. Matekoni moved towards the car and opened the driver's door. He would never mention the fact to Mma Mateleke, but he did not like her car. He found it difficult to put his finger on it, but there was something about it that he distrusted. Now, sitting in the driver's seat and turning the key in the ignition, he had a very strong sense that he was up against electronics. In the old days—as Mr. J.L.B. Matekoni called everything that took place more than ten years ago—you would never have had to bother very much about electronics, but now, with so many cars concealing computer chips in their engines, it was a different matter. "You should take this car to a computer shop," he had been tempted to say on a number of occasions. "It is really a computer, you know."

The ignition was, as Mma Mateleke had reported, quite unresponsive. Sighing, he leaned under the dashboard to find the lever that would open the bonnet, but there was no lever. He turned to unwind the window so that he could ask Mma Mateleke where the lever was, but the windows, being electric, would not work. He opened the door.

"How do you get at the engine on this car?" he asked. "I can't see the lever."

"That is because there is no lever," she replied. "There is a button. There in the middle. Look."

He saw the button, with its small graphic portrayal of a car bonnet upraised. He pressed it; nothing happened.

"It is dead too," said Mma Mateleke, in a matter-of-fact voice. "The whole car has died."

Mr. J.L.B. Matekoni climbed out of the car. "I will get it open somehow," he said. "There is always some way round these things." He was not sure that there was.

Mr. Ntirang now spoke. "I think that it is time for me to get on with my journey," he said. "You are in very good hands now, Mma. The best hands in Gaborone, people say."

Mr. J.L.B. Matekoni was a modest man, but was clearly pleased with the compliment. He smiled at Mr. Ntirang, almost, if not completely, ready to forgive him his earlier display of bad driving. He noticed, though, an exchange of glances between Mma Mateleke and Mr. Ntirang, glances that were difficult to read. Was there reproach—just a hint of reproach—on Mma Mateleke's part? But why should she have anything over which to reproach this man who had stopped to see that she was all right?

Mr. Ntirang took a step back towards his car. "Goodbye, Rra," he said. "And I hope that you get to the bottom of this problem. I'm sure you will."

Mr. J.L.B. Matekoni watched as the other man got into his car and drove off. He was interested in the car, which was an expensive model, of a sort that one saw only rarely. He wondered what the engine would look like, mentally undressing the car. Mechanics did that sometimes: as some men will imagine a woman without her clothes, so they will picture a car engine without its surrounding metal; guilty pleasures both. He was so engaged in this that Mr. Ntirang was well on his way before Mr. J.L.B. Matekoni realised that the red car was being driven back to Gaborone. Mma Mateleke had said, quite unambiguously, that Mr. Ntirang had been on his way to Lobatse, and Mr. Ntirang had nodded—equally unambiguously—to confirm that this was indeed true. Yet here he was, driving back in the direction from which he had come. Had he forgotten where he was going? Could anybody be so forgetful as to fail to remember that they were driving from Gaborone to Lobatse, and not the other way round? The answer was that of course they could: Mr. J.L.B. Matekoni himself had an aunt who had set out to drive to Serowe but who had turned back halfway because she had forgotten why it was that she wanted to go to Serowe in the first place. But he did not think it likely that Mr. Ntirang was liable to such absent-mindedness. It was his driving style that pointed to this conclusion—he was a man who very clearly knew where he was going.

CHAPTER TWO

TEAPOTS AND EFFICIENCY

MMA MATELEKE may not have been endowed with great mechanical knowledge, but her assessment that there was no life left in her engine proved to be quite correct.

"You see," she said, as they settled down to the trip back to Gaborone, her car travelling behind them like a half-welcome hitchhiker, its front wheels hoisted up on the back of the towing truck, "you see, I was right about the engine. Dead. And what am I going to do now, Mr. J.L.B. Matekoni? How am I going to cope with no car? What if somebody starts to have a baby, and I have to wait for a minibus to come along? And the minibus says, 'We're not going that way, Mma, but we can drop you nearby.' What then? You can't say to a mother, 'Please wait, Mma, until I get a minibus that is going near you.' You can't say that because I can tell you one thing, Rra, that I've learned over the last fifteen years. One thing. And that thing is that you cannot tell a baby when is the right time to come into this world. That is something the baby decides."

Mr. J.L.B. Matekoni listened politely. He knew that Mma Mateleke had a tendency to talk at great length; indeed, he could always tell when Mma Ramotswe had been to see her friend because she inevitably came back not only exhausted but also disinclined to say very much. "Mma Mateleke has done all my talking for me today," she once said. "I cannot say anything more until tomorrow. Or maybe the day after that. It has all been said."

Mma Mateleke looked out of the window. They were passing a road that led off to the west, one of those rough, dirt roads that was more holes than surface, but which had served people and cattle, as well as the occasional wild animal, year after year. It had served, and would continue to do so until it was washed away in some heavier-than-usual rainy season, and people would forget that anybody ever went that way. "That road," observed Mma Mateleke, "goes to a place where there is a woman I know well, Rra. And why do I know this woman well? Because she has had fifteen children, can you believe it? Fifteen. And fourteen of them are still here—only one is late. That one, he ate a battery, Rra, and became late quite quickly after that. He was not right in the head."

Mr. J.L.B. Matekoni frowned. Was eating a battery always fatal, or did it depend on the battery? Did it matter if the battery was charged, or flat? These were the questions that popped up in his mind, but he knew that they were the questions a man would ask and a woman would not, and he should not raise them. So he confined himself to saying, "That is very sad, Mma. Even if you have sixteen children, it is still sad to lose one."

"Fifteen," corrected Mma Mateleke, in a rather schoolmarmish way. "She had fifteen, and now has fourteen. And no husband, by the way. All the children are by different fathers."

Mr. J.L.B. Matekoni shook his head. "That is very wrong," he said.

"Yes," agreed Mma Mateleke. "What happened to marriage, Mr. J.L.B. Matekoni?"

"I am married," he said. "I am very much in favour of it." He paused. He was thinking of what he had witnessed at the site of the breakdown. What was that man—Mr. Ntirang or whatever he was called—what was he doing coming down to see that Mma Mateleke was all right? He recalled what he had imagined Mma Ramotswe might have said, had he told her about Mr. Ntirang's bad driving: *That man is having an affair.* Was he? Was that why he was rushing down to Lobatse, to meet his lover—none other than Mma Mateleke?

He glanced at Mma Mateleke, sitting beside him. She was an attractive woman, he decided, although an unduly talkative woman would never have appealed to him personally. Yet there were some men who liked that sort of woman, who got nothing but pleasure from listening to the incessant chatter of their wife or girlfriend. Some men even found that exciting in a physical way . . . He bit his lip. He could not imagine being interested in that way in somebody like Mma Mateleke; how would one ever get to plant a kiss on such a person if she was always talking? It would be difficult to get one's lips into contact with a mouth that was always opening and shutting to form words; that would surely be very distracting for a man, he thought, and might even discourage him to the point of disinclination, if that was the right word. But it did not do to think about these things, he felt; it was no business of his whether or not Mma Mateleke was having an affair with Mr. Ntirang, and this was not even altered by the fact that she was married—apparently happily—to a part-time reverend, of all people. This reverend was popular and highly thought of, and even broadcast every now and then on Radio Botswana, when he would talk on a programme called *From the Pulpit.* It is no business of mine, thought Mr. J.L.B. Matekoni; my business is to fix cars, just as it is Mma Mateleke's business to bring babies into the world.

No, it was none of his business to speculate, but he could still ask Mma Mateleke how her husband was, which he did, and she replied, "My husband is in very good health, thank you, Rra."

The answer came quickly, and Mr. J.L.B. Matekoni found himself wondering whether it was not perhaps a little bit on the dismissive side, as if she wished to preclude any further discussion of the reverend. The words *thank you* can sometimes be uttered in that way, meaning *No further discussion, please,* as in: *I am quite all right, thank you very much.*

"I am glad to hear that he is well," he said. "That is good."

"Yes," said Mma Mateleke. "That is good."

There was a silence. Mr. J.L.B. Matekoni took the opportunity to wind down the window on the driver's side. Then he said, "He must be very busy. A popular reverend is always busy, isn't he? Even if he is part-time."

Mma Mateleke nodded. She was looking out of the window on her side. "There is always something happening," she said. "People forget that he is part-time, and that he has a business to run as well. They get married and die and do all these things that need reverends. And he has to think about what he is going to say in his sermons on the radio. That is very hard work, of course, because you cannot go on the radio and say any old thing, can you?"

He shook his head. "That is very true. You cannot say the first thing in your mind when you know that the whole country is listening."

"*If* it's listening," said Mma Mateleke. "I think there are many people who turn off the radio when my husband's programme comes on."

Mr. J.L.B. Matekoni frowned. This was a strange thing for a wife to say; surely if one's spouse was on the radio one should be a bit more loyal in one's remarks. It was a very odd remark, but he decided to make light of it. "Those will be the bad people," he said. "Bad people do not like to listen to reverends on the radio. They make them feel guilty. So all the bad people turn off at the same time—click, click, click."

He looked at her sideways, expecting her to laugh, or at least smile, at his observation. But she did not. She was looking out of the window again, and he was not sure that she had heard him.

"It is his birthday next week," she said suddenly. "I shall make him a very special cake. He is turning forty, you see, and I am planning a special party for him."

Mr. J.L.B. Matekoni felt relieved. That settled that, he thought. If Mma Mateleke were having an affair, then she would hardly be talking about making a special effort for her husband's birthday. This was not the way a woman in that situation behaved. He felt guilty about his suspicions; if everybody who saw a married woman talking to a strange man were to draw the conclusion that there was something going on, then ordinary life would become quite impossible. He would be unable to talk to Mma Makutsi, for example, and she to him. And Mma Ramotswe would be unable to talk to the apprentices—especially Charlie, whom any husband might very readily assume was up to no good, with those shoes of his and the sunglasses that he affected, even on an overcast day and, as Mr. J.L.B. Matekoni had once observed, at night. No, there was nothing at all to justify any suspicions, and he should stop thinking this way. And yet . . . why had Mma Mateleke's friend changed course so readily from Lobatse to Gaborone? No matter which way he looked at it, that did not make sense. He would talk to Mma Ramotswe; she knew about these things, and if there was an innocent explanation— which surely there must be—she could be expected to find it.

AS MR. J.L.B. MATEKONI was driving Mma Mateleke and her unresponsive car back to Gaborone, in the offices of the No. 1 Ladies' Detective Agency Mma Makutsi, assistant detective and graduate summa cum laude of the Botswana Secretarial College, was busy making the mid-morning tea. As usual, she was preparing red bush tea for her employer and ordinary tea for herself, using a special teapot for each purpose. The two teapots were the same colour, an indeterminate brown, but there was a distinguishing feature: Mma Ramotswe's teapot was considerably larger. Mma Makutsi, who had been used all her life to having very little, and accepted this with the quiet resignation that such people often possess, had never questioned this arrangement. Mma Ramotswe was, after all, the proprietor of the agency, and the owner of both pots. But she had recently asked herself whether it would not make more sense for the red bush tea, which was required in smaller quantities, to be brewed in the smaller teapot, while the ordinary tea might be made in the larger pot, since it was not only for her own consumption, but was also drunk by Mr. J.L.B. Matekoni, by his unqualified assistant, Mr. Polopetsi, and by the two apprentices, Charlie and Fanwell. It was unusual for all of these to present themselves for tea at the same time, but it sometimes did happen. Then it was necessary for Mma Makutsi to brew another pot, while the resources of Mma Ramotswe's commodious teapot were barely called upon.

She had been silent, but now she decided to broach the subject. At the Botswana Secretarial College, where she had obtained the hitherto unheard-of result of ninety-seven per cent in the final examinations, Mma Makutsi had been taught that it was always better to raise issues of office procedure rather than to brood over them. "There is nothing worse, ladies, than muttering about something," said the lecturer. "If something is wrong, then raise it. Not only is that better for you—nursing a grudge makes you far less efficient in your work—but it is also much better for your boss. So spit it out, and always remember this: a problem shared is a problem solved." Or had she said, *A problem shared is a problem halved?* It was difficult to remember these things when there were so many proverbs jostling to give advice. *Locusts do not land only on the land that belongs to your neighbour. The person who lies by the fire knows how hot it is* . . . And so on; all of these sayings were undoubtedly true, but might still quite easily be forgotten—until the moment you found yourself doing exactly the thing that the proverb warned you against.

Perhaps there was a saying warning you against questioning the size of another's teapot; something like, *A teapot is only as large as it needs to be,* or *Do not talk about the size of another's teapot when* . . . No, this was nonsense, Mma Makutsi decided, and there was no reason at all why she should not raise the matter with Mma Ramotswe, who was reasonable, after all, and full of proverbs too.

"I've been thinking," she began.

Mma Ramotswe looked up from her desk. She smiled. "Thinking? We all have a lot to think about, I suppose."

Mma Makutsi busied herself with the kettle. "Yes, Mma. You know how sometimes a good idea comes to you? You don't necessarily think about it deliberately, but it just comes. And there you have your idea."

"Yes," said Mma Ramotswe. "And what idea do you have, Mma Makutsi? I'm sure it will be a good one." She was always polite—and encouraging too; a lesser employer might have said, *Thinking? There is work to do, Mma!* Or, even more discouragingly, *I am the one to do the thinking round here, Mma!*

Mma Makutsi glanced at Mma Ramotswe. There was no trace of sarcasm in her voice; Mma Ramotswe did not believe in sarcasm. "This idea is about teapots. About efficiency and tea-pots. Yes, it's about those two things."

"Good," said Mma Ramotswe. "Anybody who could invent a more efficient teapot would be doing a great service to . . ." She paused, before concluding: "to all tea-drinking people."

Mma Makutsi swallowed; sometimes it was easier to deal with a hostile reaction rather than a welcoming one. "Well, I don't think I could invent a new teapot, Mma. I am not that sort of person. But—"

Mma Ramotswe interrupted her with a laugh. "Anybody can invent something, Mma. Even you and I—we might invent something. You do not have to be a scientist to invent something very important. Some inventions just happen. Penicillin. You know about that?"

Mma Makutsi saw the conversation drifting away from teapots. "I was wondering . . ."

"We were taught about penicillin in school," Mma Ramotswe mused. "At Mochudi. We were taught about the man who found penicillin growing in . . ." She tailed off. Again, it was hard to remember, even if she could see herself quite clearly in the school on the top of the kopje overlooking Mochudi, with the morning sun coming through the window, illuminating in its shafts of light the little flecks of floating dust; and the voice of the teacher telling them about the great inventions that had changed the world. Everything, all these great things, had happened so far away—or so it seemed to her at the time. The world was made to sound as if it belonged to other people—to those who lived in dis-tant countries that were so different from Botswana; that was before people had learned to assert that the world was theirs too, that what happened in Botswana was every bit as important, and valuable, as what happened anywhere else.

But where had that doctor grown the penicillin that was to

save so many lives? In his garden? She thought not. It was in his laboratory somewhere, perhaps in a cup of tea that he left on a windowsill, as Mr. J.L.B. Matekoni had done once and Mma Ramotswe had discovered it, months later, when the half-finished liquid had turned to green mould.

"In a cup of tea," she said hesitantly. "Maybe. Or in a saucer, perhaps."

"That is very interesting, Mma," said Mma Makutsi briskly. "But I have been thinking about a more efficient way of making the tea in this office. I am not interested in making penicillin or inventing anything."

Mma Ramotswe nodded encouragingly. "It is a good thing to be efficient," she said.

Mma Makutsi seized her chance. "So why don't we use the big teapot to make the ordinary tea," she said. "There are always more people wanting ordinary tea—Mr. Polopetsi, for instance, and Charlie and Fanwell. If we made the ordinary tea in that big pot, then I would not have to make a second pot." She paused. "And it would make no difference to your red bush tea, Mma. You would still have more than enough."

For a few moments Mma Ramotswe said nothing. *I've offended her,* thought Mma Makutsi. *I shouldn't have spoken about this.* But then Mma Ramotswe, who had been looking out of the window, as if pondering this casually lobbed bombshell, turned to Mma Makutsi and smiled. "That is a very good idea, Mma," she said. "Every business needs new ideas, and that is one. Change the pots next time you make tea." She paused. "I do not mind having the smaller pot. Not at all." And then, after a further pause, "Even if I have always loved that big teapot."

"Then you must still have it," said Mma Makutsi quickly. "Efficiency isn't the only thing, Mma."

Mma Ramotswe shook her head. "No, what you said, Mma,

is quite right. There is no point in filling a big teapot with red bush tea if I am the only one who drinks it. I do not want to be selfish."

You are never selfish, thought Mma Makutsi, ruefully. Never. I am the selfish one. "But I did not mean to take it from you," she said. And she tried to explain: this was no act of petty office self-aggrandisement; it was not that. Nor was it the act of a bored bureaucrat, of one of those who sought to bring about change in the well-ordered ways of others simply because they had to find something to do. It was not that, either. "I am not one of those people who change everything just to make it more efficient."

"I know you aren't," said Mma Ramotswe. "But you are still right."

Mma Makutsi, in her misery, looked down at her shoes, as she often did at such moments. She was wearing her everyday footwear—a pair of brown shoes with rather frayed edges, shoes that had the look of experience. They looked back at her with that slight air of superiority that her shoes tended to effect. *Don't look at us, Boss,* the shoes said. *It was your big idea, not ours. We don't go around trying to change things, do we? We do not.*

AS IT HAPPENED, there were few takers for tea that morning, as the mechanics were busier than usual and unable to take the time off. An hour or so later, though, Charlie came in to report that he was going out to fetch a spare part for Mr. J.L.B. Matekoni, and would be happy to see if there was any mail in the mailbox near the Riverside filling station. His offer was accepted, and he returned twenty minutes later with a bundle of letters, which he placed on Mma Ramotswe's desk.

"There is only one interesting letter there," he said. "It is from a place in the United States. I can tell from the stamp. Wow! One, two, three!"

Mma Makutsi looked at him with irritation. "It is none of your business," she said. "Our letters are none of your business, Charlie. You are just a mechanic—not a detective." Her irritation suddenly changed to pleasure as she contemplated her next observation. "Actually, you are just an apprentice, not a proper mechanic yet."

It was a telling blow. Charlie and Fanwell had not made great progress with their apprenticeships, largely because of their failure to apply themselves to the regular examinations that the Apprenticeship Board required. Fanwell, at least, had an excuse for this, as he was chronically dyslexic and, although intelligent, had difficulty understanding examination questions. Charlie, who was both intelligent and a quick reader, could claim only fecklessness as an excuse, if it were an excuse, which of course it was not.

"It is addressed to Mma Ramotswe," he snapped. "Not to you."

Mma Ramotswe made a calming gesture; she did not like the arguments that seemed to flare up between these two, nor any arguments, for that matter. "I do not mind," she muttered as she extracted the white airmail letter from the pile of manila envelopes.

Charlie threw a triumphant glance towards Mma Makutsi. "You must be very proud, Mma," he said. "You must be proud that there are people there who know about you and are writing to you. Nobody in America knows about her over there. She is an unknown lady, Mma; you are very well known."

"Ssh, Charlie," said Mma Ramotswe. "I am sure that there are many people there who know about Mma Makutsi. Or they will in future, I am certain of it."

She slit open the letter and began to read it. They watched her, and at the end she said, "Oh dear, I am very sorry. This is very sad, but also it is very good news for one man."

CHAPTER THREE

MARRIED, LIKE DOVES

So, MMA RAMOTSWE," said Mr. J.L.B. Matekoni. "So you received a big letter today."

They were sitting on the veranda at Zebra Drive at that companionable hour when the late afternoon shades almost imperceptibly into early evening. The sky was not yet dark, but had become paler, and pinker, too, in the west. Dusk was not far off, but had not yet made its softening mark; yet the birds knew, and were flying from tree to tree restlessly, finding just the right place to spend the impending night. A pair of Cape turtle doves, as married as the couple sitting on the veranda, edged closer to one another on the bough of the acacia tree that sheltered part of Mr. J.L.B. Matekoni's vegetable garden. Their anxious cooing could be heard alongside the sound of a car making its way home to a neighbouring house, the half-hearted barking of a neighbour's dog, the sound of a radio somewhere indeterminate.

Mr. J.L.B. Matekoni, unusually for him, was drinking a beer. He drank very little, and Mma Ramotswe hardly at all, but on the occasional evening he would unwind with a glass of Lion lager, savouring the feel of the damp, cold glass against his hand almost as much as the freshening sharpness of the beer. Mma Ramotswe would sometimes accompany him, as she did now, taking a tea-spoon of beer—a single teaspoon—and putting it into a glass of water with a slice of lemon. The resulting concoction she would sip at, convinced that even this quite homeopathic dilution would go to her head if consumed too quickly.

They had raised their glasses to one another in salute, and then he had asked his question about the letter. Charlie had mentioned it that morning as they were attending to a recalci-trant gearbox, but he had not known what the letter contained. "Big news, I think, Boss," he had said. "A letter from America means a big case."

And now Mma Ramotswe said, "Yes, I had a letter."

He waited for her to reveal more. He would not pry; they might share the same roof, and the same bed, but they both understood the idea of professional confidence, at least in rela-tion to the real secrets that were bared to Mma Ramotswe in the course of her work—the admissions and accusations of adultery, the doubts about others, the frank tragedies of betrayal. But this letter, it transpired, contained nothing like that.

"It was from a man in America," Mma Ramotswe said, lifting her glass to sip at her drink.

"Oh yes?"

"Yes. From a lawyer, Rra."

Mr. J.L.B. Matekoni frowned. Letters from lawyers were not always welcomed, especially when received by mechanics. It was very strange, he thought: a lawyer's letter was capable of striking fear into the strongest of hearts, yet who worried about a letter from a mechanic . . . They should, of course: mechanics' letters could be devastating—*I have examined your car, and I regret to inform you that . . .* Mechanics could be the conveyors of the most serious news, but they normally chose to give such news face-to-face. And on such occasions a suitably grave expression was required; one should not give bad mechanical news lightly, as Mr. J.L.B. Matekoni had felt obliged to warn his apprentices. He had overheard Charlie telling a woman that her car was *finished,* and on another occasion the young man had told a client that his brakes were the worst brakes in Botswana, adding, *And I've seen some pretty bad brakes in my time!* No, that was not the professional way, not that those young men understood what professionalism was all about.

Mma Ramotswe expanded on the contents of the letter. "This lawyer, this man in a place called St. Paul—that is a good name, isn't it, Rra? St. Paul must be a good place to live—this man said that he is writing on behalf of a lady who is now late. He said that she was his client and his good friend, and that now that she is late, he is looking after her affairs."

"Her executor," said Mr. J.L.B. Matekoni.

"Yes, her executor. And it is because he is her executor that he has to find a certain person in Botswana."

Mr. J.L.B. Matekoni looked down into his beer. "Because that person owes money?" he asked. It would be a typical case, he thought; although the Government of Botswana very rarely borrowed money, the same could not be said of the people themselves, especially at the end of the month, just before pay day, when everyone's pockets would be empty. It was very common then for people to seek a loan from some sympathetic friend or neighbour, or, if their luck was in, from a stranger whom they might never see again. It was not a grave failing—there were many worse—but it was a failing nonetheless. So somebody had borrowed money from an American visitor, and then the visitor had gone home and died and his executor had to look for the debtor to get the loan repaid. That was obviously what had happened here, and now Mma Ramotswe had to find this person and reclaim the money. Some chance of that, thought Mr. J.L.B. Matekoni . . .

Mma Ramotswe laughed. "No. I can tell what you're thinking, but no. This is the other way round. The lawyer wants to *give* this person some money."

Mr. J.L.B. Matekoni's expression showed his surprise. "You mean that the American person borrowed money from this Motswana? And now the lawyer wants to repay the debt?"

"I do not mean that," said Mma Ramotswe. "I am talking about a legacy, Rra. That is nothing to do with borrowing, that is to do with gifts. This late person in America wants to make a gift to a person in Botswana. It is a legacy."

"Ah." Mr. J.L.B. Matekoni understood perfectly. Mma Ramotswe had received a legacy of cattle on the death of her father, and he had once been left a bequest of five hundred pula from a grateful client who had declared that Mr. J.L.B. Matekoni was the only person who understood his car. Any news of a legacy was welcome news indeed.

She told him about the letter, hearing in her mind once more the precise phrases in the beautifully typed letter (Mma Makutsi might take note of the spacing; but that was another matter, and would not be mentioned now).

Dear Mrs. Ramotswe,

You will forgive, I hope, this approach without an introduction: your name has been given to me by the American Embassy in Gaborone with the assurance that you are the most appropriate person for me to consult on this unusual matter.

The late Mrs. Estelle Grant died about six months ago. I was her lawyer for many years, and, I might add, her friend. She was a fine woman, who was much appreciated in this city and beyond. It is not surprising that her will contained a number of charitable bequests, as she was an ardent supporter of many causes in this country and abroad.

Under the terms of the will I have been appointed her executor. As you will no doubt know, it is the job of an executor to implement the wishes of the testator, the person whose will it is. Sometimes this is difficult, as the instructions left may be obscure or difficult to apply. In my long experience as a lawyer, I have seen quite a number of bequests fail because it has been impossible to work out what the testator meant.

But even if there is ambiguity or obscurity, an executor must do his best to bring about the result that the deceased wanted. This is a sacred trust, in a sense: we must do our best to honour the last wishes of those who have left us—provided, of course, that such last wishes are consonant with good morals and standards of decency.

Mrs. Grant's will has proved relatively easy to put into effect. But although I have been able to identify and pay most of the beneficiaries of her bequests, I have been left with one that I feel is going to be more difficult. That is the one that I am writing to you about, with a view to engaging your services to help me identify the person who is entitled to the bequest in question. That person, I believe, lives in your country.

Please allow me to explain. Mrs. Grant was not a great traveller. I was aware of the fact that she visited Jamaica ten years ago, and had made two or three trips to Europe over the years. One special trip she did make, though, was to Botswana, which she visited exactly four years ago, in the month of June or possibly July. Some time around then. I knew about this trip because she spoke to me about it. She also showed me the pictures she had taken, and I must say that I was most impressed with the beauty of your country.

It was more than simple natural beauty that impressed Mrs. Grant. In addition to that, she was very taken with the kindness of the people whom she encountered. She talked to me about this on more than one occasion, saying that she had never before come across such warmth and courtesy being shown to strangers. I believe that this affected her very deeply.

I am sorry to say that about nine months ago Mrs. Grant fell ill. The diagnosis was not a good one, and although she remained lucid and composed, I think that her end was not an altogether easy one. I visited her regularly, and we talked about many things. It is strange how the imminence of death can either focus the conversation between two peo-ple, or can render them curiously mute. In our case, many things were said that had remained unsaid during the course of our friendship. In particular, we reflected on the fact that although we had both lost our spouses some years earlier, it had not occurred to us to change our friend-ship into marriage. And now it was too late, as it often is. (Please forgive me for recounting these somewhat personal matters—I do so, I think, because the person at the Em-bassy who recommended you said to me that you were a sympathetic and understanding woman.)

It was on one of my visits to Mrs. Grant in the hospital that she said to me that there was an extra provision that she wanted me to draft for her will. I did this there and then, using nurses as witnesses, as it is my firm belief that one should never lose time in putting into writing a client's verbal instructions relating to a will. I was right, as it hap-pened: Mrs. Grant died two days later.

That day in the hospital, Mrs. Grant told me a story. She said that when she had gone to Botswana she had visited, as many do, the Okavango Delta. She had gone, again as so many others do, to a safari camp on the edge of the river and had stayed there for four days. I knew all about this, of course, as she had already told me of that visit. What I did not know, though, was that there was a guide there who had been particularly kind to her. He had taken her on a bush walk and had gone to great trouble to locate a lioness that they had been able to observe from a safe distance. She said that this guide had gone out of his way to make her visit a memorable one. *In his eyes,* she said, *I was probably a passerby from a remote place, but that made no difference. He treated me as if I were a member of his family, an aunt perhaps. There is an expression, "the kindness of strangers": well, I encountered it very vividly during those days.*

Mrs. Grant told me that it was her wish to send a gift to this man. She had meant to write and thank him, but had put it off and put it off, as we often do with such good intentions. Now, in the face of death, she wanted to tie up loose ends, and this was one such. She wanted to thank this man and send him a gift of money. This, she instructed me, was to be the sum of three thousand dollars.

Naturally, I asked for details, so that I could put them into the provision I was drawing up for the will. Unfortunately she could not remember the guide's name nor, I very much regret to say, the exact name of the camp. All that she was able to say to me was that the camp bore the name of a bird or an animal. And so I had to draft a provision that left the money "to the guide who took such care of me in Botswana," and to leave the rest for further investigation. That investigation is what I would like you to undertake on my behalf: please locate the camp and find out the name of the man who looked after her. I should not imagine that this will be too difficult. The estate will, of course, meet all expenses and pay such fees as you may reasonably charge. Please confirm that you can undertake this work, and send me a note of your fee rate.

Finally, may I say, Mrs. Ramotswe, that although this seems like a strange request, it is by no means a light or whimsical one. Mrs. Grant was a woman who believed that goodness in this life should not go unrewarded; she was also a fine judge of men. If she said that this guide who looked after her was a good man, then you may rest assured that he was. I am sure, if and when we find him, we shall discover that he deserves this recognition of what he did.

I have enclosed with this letter a copy of Mrs. Grant's obituary from the local paper. It has a nice photograph of her and it tells you about her life, which was a good one, as you will see.

I remain, yours truly,

Oliver J. Maxwell

"But what if he isn't?" asked Mr. J.L.B. Matekoni.

The question took Mma Ramotswe by surprise. "But what if who isn't what?"

Mr. J.L.B. Matekoni looked out over the garden. "What if this guide—whatever his name turns out to be—what if he isn't a good man at all? He said—this Mr. Oliver J. Maxwell—that we will find that this man deserves the money. But what if he doesn't?"

Mma Ramotswe thought for a moment. It was not unlike Mr. J.L.B. Matekoni to come up with a seemingly simple observation that could turn quite quickly into a profound and complicated question. It was, she conceded, perfectly possible that the guide was not what Mma Grant thought he was: people who look after visitors—hotel people, waiters, and the like—can appear charming on the surface, but only because their job requires that of them. She herself had seen this with one of the waitresses at the café that she frequented at the Riverview shopping centre. It was a good place to sit, affording a ringside seat of all the comings and goings that took place in the car park and around the small craft market that had sprung up, and she had got to know all the waitresses by now. She had found them very helpful and pleasant, but then she had seen one of them mocking a customer behind her back. The episode had not lasted for long, but she had spotted it and then looked away, out of shame for the young woman who was making fun of the customer. Mma Ramotswe had felt outraged. It was the sort of thing that would never have happened in her father's Botswana, that Botswana in which young people had shown respect for older people, not out of fear or for any other craven reason, but simply because they had lived longer and had acquired something that could only be described as wisdom. Yes, wisdom: that was something that came to everybody, although it came in varying quantities and at different times. Wisdom, which was an understanding of the feelings of others and of what would work and what would not work; which stood by one's shoulder and said this is right or this is wrong, or this person is lying or this person is telling the truth. And now here was this waitress, who was seventeen, perhaps, pulling a face and imitating the expression of that harmless woman who, admittedly, was wearing a dress that was quite unsuitable for one of her figure—such legs should not be displayed, even in modern Botswana—and what if that poor woman heard the giggling and turned round and saw herself being parodied?

Wildlife guides, of course, were in a different class from

seventeen-year-old waitresses; they were experienced people
who had undergone rigorous training and passed the Wildlife
Department's legendarily difficult examinations. They had to
know the names of all the plants and which animals ate them and
which ones could be used for medicines. They had to be able to
read the ground and tell from among the myriad markings in the
sand which creature had passed that way, and when. Here the
S-shaped trail of a snake; here the tiny footprint of a dassie; here
the place where the elephant had snapped the half-grown acacia
as if it were matchwood. And they had to know the history of
Botswana too, in case they were asked by their clients to explain
something. *Where was Bechuanaland? Who was Seretse Khama?
When did they first discover diamonds in Botswana? And, tell me,
who was Robert Moffat?* There was so much to know, and anybody
who knew all that surely would have more than his fair share of
wisdom, and would hardly be one to be dismissive or insincere in
his dealings with visitors.

"I think that we shall find that he is a good man, this guide,"
she said.

Mr. J.L.B. Matekoni looked doubtful. He did not think that
the mere fact that one was a qualified guide meant that one
would be worthy of a gift of three thousand dollars. "Well," he
said, "you may be right or you may be wrong. But just think for a
moment: What happens if you find that you are wrong, and that
he is not a good man? What then?"

"We give him the money," said Mma Ramotswe. "Or, rather,
we send his name and address to the lawyer and he sends him
three thousand dollars. I am not a court of law, Mr. J.L.B.
Matekoni, and it is not for me to make a judgement on whether
anybody deserves anything. In this matter I am really only a . . ."
She searched for the right metaphor. "I am really only a postman.
That is what I am."

Mr. J.L.B. Matekoni sighed. "I see. And I suppose you're right, Mma. I do not sit in judgement on my clients' cars—every car receives the same consideration."

"Well, there you are," she said. "I have finished my drink now, and the children will have done their homework. They will be getting hungry, I think."

Mr. J.L.B. Matekoni lifted his glass and drained the last of his beer. "Before you start cooking," he said, "I have something to tell you. I did not get a letter today, but I did see something rather strange. Your friend, Mma Mateleke—well, her car broke down on the Lobatse Road and I went off to deal with it, and . . ."

CHAPTER FOUR

A MAN'S FACE IS LIKE
THE VERY LAND

THAT SAME EVENING, while Mma Ramotswe was cooking dinner in her house on Zebra Drive, Mma Makutsi was preparing a special stew for her fiancé, Mr. Phuti Radiphuti, owner of the Double Comfort Furniture Shop. Phuti Radiphuti had shown himself to be a creature of habit, eating with senior relatives on certain fixed nights of the week, and then with Mma Makutsi on others. Mma Makutsi did not mind this too much—she would have preferred for him to have had dinner at her house every night, but she knew that it was only a matter of time before they were married and then this would happen anyway. Of course, there was always a chance that he would expect to continue with his peripatetic meal habits, but she would deal with that tactfully if the situation arose. She would be prepared to receive his senior aunt for the occasional meal, no more frequently than would be expected of a duteous wife, but she was not having that woman claiming more than her fair share of Phuti's company. There was no doubt in Mma Makutsi's mind that when a man married, his obligations to his female relatives, particularly those owed to distant female relatives, were eclipsed by the claims of his wife. But there would be opportunity enough to sort that out once the marriage had taken place. For the time being, the existing routine could be observed and, for her part, tolerated.

Men were strange, thought Mma Makutsi. There were plenty of people who held that there was no material difference between men and women, but such people, she believed, were simply wrong. Of course men and women were different, and women were, on the whole, different in a better way. That was not to put men down—Mma Makutsi did not believe in doing that—it was simply a realistic recognition of the fact that women were capable of doing rather more than men. In fact, thought Mma Makutsi, there was a lot of truth in Mma Ramotswe's insight that while men still claimed so many of the top jobs, it was actually women who were running everything in the background. Men needed those top jobs to make them feel good, so that they could imagine they were in control, while all the time it was women who were in the driving seat.

She had considered this observation. "Perhaps," she had said to Mma Ramotswe, "perhaps . . ."

Of course, men were getting better—that was another fact Mma Ramotswe had pointed out to her, and with which she was strongly inclined to agree. Old-fashioned men—men who could do very little about the house and could talk about nothing but cattle and football—such men were increasingly being replaced by men who had many more interests and topics of conversation. These *new men*, as she had seen them referred to, were not only prepared to talk about many of the things that women liked, but they also took a strong interest in clothes. One or two of them, she had heard, even put cosmetics on their faces, which Mma Makutsi, open as she was to new developments, thought was going too far. "There's nothing much men can do about their faces," she once said to Mma Ramotswe. And Mma Ramotswe, immediately recognising the truth of this, had said, "No, Mma, that is quite true. Men's faces are very unfortunate. They can do nothing."

This remark sounded somewhat uncharitable, and Mma Ramotswe had quickly added: "Of course, that is not men's fault. And there is something reassuring about a man's face. It's . . . it's like the land, I think. It's always there."

They looked at one another doubtfully, and tacitly agreed to defer until later any further discussion of men's faces, and indeed the broader topic of men and women; such issues were never easily resolved, and no matter how readily men's characteristics suggested themselves for scrutiny, at the end of the day men simply *were,* and most, if not all, women seemed to be thankful for that.

Mma Makutsi was certainly grateful for Phuti Radiphuti. He had come into her life at an unexpected moment, when she was almost at the point of reconciling herself to the possibility that she might never find anybody suitable. That would have been a bleak conclusion for anybody to reach, and particularly somebody as young as Mma Makutsi. But one had to be realistic, and there seemed to be few men apparently interested in a woman with problematic skin and large glasses. Most men, it appeared, were more interested in the likes of Violet Sephotho, the arch-Jezebel who had graduated with barely fifty per cent from the Botswana Secretarial College. She it was who had shamelessly attempted to win Phuti from Mma Makutsi by insinuating herself into a job at the Double Comfort Furniture Shop, in the bed department, of all departments—how appropriate and inappropriate at the same time—and had, thankfully, failed. Violet would have shown not the slightest scrap of interest in Phuti had she not realised that he was a wealthy man. That changed everything in her book: How could she be indifferent to a man who was due to inherit a large furniture shop *and* the large herd of cattle built up by his father, the very elderly but not quite yet late Mr. Radiphuti Senior?

The material comfort that Phuti offered had not been a consideration for Mma Makutsi. Indeed, when she had met him at that fateful first session of the Botswana Academy of Dance and Movement, she had been unaware of who he was and what he possessed. All she knew was that here was a man with a very bad stutter and a marked lack of dancing ability. For a few brief moments she had felt a certain irritation at the fact that he had been designated as her partner, particularly with Violet Sephotho smirking at her with her elegant, deft-of-foot partner, but her impatience had quickly been replaced by sympathy. There was something gentle about this man with his awkward ways, and that could not but appeal to a woman. Affection and friendship had grown into something else, and she had come to appreciate and love Phuti more than she had ever loved any man. Such romantic feelings as she had experienced before were mere shallow infatuations when compared with the emotions that now overcame her. *Mrs. Grace Radiphuti,* she said to herself, savouring each word and its delicious associations; *wife of Mr. Phuti Radiphuti, Assistant Detective.* No, that was wrong; she, not Phuti, was the assistant detective. *Mrs. Grace Radiphuti, Dip. Sec., Assistant Detective, wife of Mr. Phuti Radiphuti.* Or even: *Mrs. Grace Radiphuti, Dip. Sec. (97), Assistant Detective, wife of Mr. Phuti Radiphuti.* The words were ripe with a sense of achievement; it was a long way from that to Bobonong, and to the days when she had had nothing, or next to nothing; when every pula, every thebe, had to be counted and made the most of. People talked of grinding poverty; well, that was exactly what poverty did—it ground.

Yet she was determined that when she married she would not

forget who she was and who her people were. She would not affect any airs. When she had gone to the Botswana Secretarial College she had been given a form to fill out, and there had been a question in it about parental occupation. She had written *Peasant* in response to that question, and she would write that again if she had occasion to answer such a question on any of the intrusive forms that various bureaucrats liked people to fill in. *I am the daughter of a peasant, and that is what I shall always be.*

She stirred the stew, glancing at her watch. Phuti was usually punctual, but every so often there would be some crisis at the furniture shop that required him to stay late at work; this might be holding him back now—some argument over invoices or a discrepancy in the till receipts, or any one of the many minor things that could interrupt the smooth workings of a furniture shop. It did not matter too much: stew did not spoil—indeed, Mma Ramotswe had once suggested to her that the older a stew the better, although within reason, of course.

But at seven o'clock she began to worry. Phuti had a mobile telephone, but Mma Makutsi did not. He had offered to buy her one, but she had declined the offer on the grounds that she did not want to impose too much, and if she had a mobile phone, she would get no peace from various relatives who had one and who would pester her with requests. So even if he had wanted to let her know that he was going to be late back, he would not have been able to do so.

The minutes passed slowly. She moved the pot to the side of the stove, where it could simmer peacefully, and untied the strings of the apron she was wearing. Then she opened the kitchen door and stepped out into her small yard. Her pawpaw tree, which had never grown straight, was outlined at its drunken angle, a dark shadow against the glow of the night sky. The light from her neighbour's uncurtained window spilled out onto the bare ground of the yard, a square of yellow; and through the window itself, a glimpse of a family seated around a table—the father, who was something in the Ministry of Telecommunications, an engineer, she thought; the mother, who worked in some lowly capacity at the diamond sorting office; and the three children, whose heads bobbed up and down above the level of the windowsill. They were never still, those children; they were always running about and throwing things and behaving as children should behave.

The lights of a car came up the road. She felt a surge of relief: she knew it was Phuti's car because one of the lights shone at a slightly different angle to the other, casting its beam more upwards than downwards. *My car needs glasses,* he had joked, and she had laughed, not because she felt that she had to, but because her fiancé said some very amusing things sometimes, and this was one of them.

The car drew to a halt outside her yard. Mma Makutsi went forward and began to open the gate, and to say, "I thought that you must be busy . . ." But then she stopped; it was not Phuti in his car but his assistant manager, Mr. Gaethele, a man with a damaged left ear.

"Phuti?" Mma Makutsi's voice was low.

Mr. Gaethele looked down. He held his hands palm outwards; a curious gesture, apologetic more than anything else; the gesture of one who has broken something, or brings news of breakage. "There has been an accident, Mma."

She stood quite still.

"He is all right, but he is in the Princess Marina. His leg is bad. You must not worry too much, Mma."

She waited for him to say something more. She could not speak. Where? How? When? There were so many questions to be asked, but she could give voice to none of them; not now, here under the pawpaw tree, to this man whom she did not know very well, who was trying to be sympathetic but was awkward in his attempt.

"I want to go and see him," she said at last, moving towards the car.

He shook his head. "No. The doctor said that we can see him tomorrow, but not until four o'clock. There is going to be an operation on his leg. His aunt is waiting at the hospital. She says that nobody else must come yet."

She stared at him, struggling to take in what had happened. She dug her fingernails into her palms, a trick she had learned at school; one pain might cancel out another, might make the world different.

"How did this thing . . ."

Mr. Gaethele shook his head. "It was one of the delivery drivers. He reversed the truck into Mr. Radiphuti. He was standing in front of small wall, and it caught his leg against the wall. Like this." He made a crushing movement with his hands.

Mma Makutsi held her hands up to her face. There would be tears, but not until she was ready to cry.

MMA RAMOTSWE did not hear about the incident at the Double Comfort Furniture Shop until the following morning. When she arrived at the office, Mma Makutsi was already there, sitting at her desk, sorting papers. As her employer entered, she did not look up, as she normally would. She was preoccupied with her work, Mma Ramotswe thought; there was nobody who could become quite as absorbed in filing papers as Mma Makutsi. Filing, she had once pronounced, is the greatest of the secretarial arts. And then she had said . . .

But something seemed not quite right, and Mma Ramotswe,

about to open the window, turned round. "There is something wrong, isn't there?"

Mma Makutsi shook her head—vigorously; so vigorously, in fact, that Mma Ramotswe's suspicions were immediately confirmed.

"There is nothing wrong. Nothing."

Mma Ramotswe left the window and crossed the room to Mma Makutsi's desk. She laid her hand on the other woman's shoulder, gently. "Mma, you can tell me."

It must be Phuti, she thought, something to do with him. There had been that problem over the negotiation of the bride price, and she did not think that it had been resolved yet. That greedy uncle from Bobonong, that man with the broken nose who had sniffed the presence of money in the Radiphuti family and had travelled all the way down from the north like a greedy vulture. It was something to do with that, obviously.

But then Mma Makutsi looked up at her and said, "Phuti is in hospital. There has been an accident." And she began to weep, dropping her head onto her forearms and rocking backwards and forwards in that curious motion that is perhaps a subconscious attempt to mimic the movement that brings comfort to a tiny baby. That we should in moments of sorrow seek to return to a time when the harshness of the world could be forfended by the simple reassurances of our parents; that we should do that . . .

"Oh, Mma Makutsi . . ."

"He is having an operation. Now, I think."

Mma Ramotswe bent forward and put both her arms around Mma Makutsi, and for a while they were silent. Then she asked what had happened, and was given the only account that the other woman had—the story as told by Mr. Gaethele.

"If it is only his leg, then that is surely not too bad."

This brought little comfort to Mma Makutsi.

"And they have the best surgeons at that hospital," said Mma Ramotswe. "They are miracle-workers."

Mma Makutsi looked at Mma Ramotswe. "But if it is only his leg, then why will they need a miracle?" She started to sob again.

Mma Ramotswe moved back to her desk. "I shall drive you to the hospital, Mma. We can go and wait there until the operation is over."

"They do not want us."

"Who says that?"

Mma Makutsi explained about the aunt and her prohibition of visitors until later that day. Mma Ramotswe, though, was not prepared to accept this; an aunt may have a role in the life of an unmarried man, but in the case of a married man—and an engaged man was as good as married in her view—aunts took second place.

"We shall go to the Princess Marina, right now. In my white van." She checked herself. "In my van." She had momentarily forgotten that the tiny white van was no more, and that its successor, mechanically superior though it might be, was no real substitute. But this was not the time for such melancholy thoughts; not when Mma Makutsi was in distress and Phuti Radiphuti, that quiet, inoffensive man who had so dramatically improved Mma Makutsi's prospects, was, for all they knew, fighting for his life in the operating theatre, or, worse still, was being wheeled out, one of the unlucky ones in that—what was it she had read?—one per cent of those who enter the theatre who do not come out alive. One in one hundred. She would not mention that figure to Mma Makutsi, for whom it might not provide the comfort that, if looked at rationally, it might be expected to provide.

CHAPTER FIVE

THEY GO TO THE HOSPITAL

THE RADIPHUTI AUNT had a face which was markedly too wide for her thin body; like a watermelon on sticks, Mma Makutsi had thought when Phuti had first shown her a photograph of her; but she had not said that, of course, remarking, instead, "You are lucky to have an aunt who loves you so much, Phuti." The impression of disproportion conveyed by this mismatch between head and body was exacerbated by feet which appeared considerably too big for the relatively spindly legs that went up into a skirt made of the brown print fabric favoured by the more conventional sort of middle-aged woman in Botswana. Mma Makutsi had only met her once before, and then briefly, but recognised her and pointed her out to Mma Ramotswe.

"That is Phuti's aunt. That is her. That lady there."

Mma Ramotswe looked in the direction indicated by Mma Makutsi. The aunt was sitting under a tree in the grounds of the hospital. Another woman, accompanied by a young girl, sat at the other end of the bench placed there. A village dog, emaciated and flyblown, lay at the girl's feet, somnolent in the growing heat of the morning, its mouth open, its preternaturally long tongue exposed to the sun.

Mma Ramotswe gestured for Mma Makutsi to follow her, although her assistant seemed anxious about doing so.

"We will speak to her," she said. "Come."

Mma Makutsi was hesitant. "She said that we should not come here until she told us. She said that . . ."

Mma Ramotswe gripped Mma Makutsi's arm. "You are the fiancée, Mma! You are almost Mrs. Radiphuti! You are the one who should be at his bedside. He will want to see you, Mma, not his aunt."

They walked towards the aunt, who turned as they approached and fixed them with a discouraging stare. Mma Ramotswe retained her grip on Mma Makutsi's arm. "Never be put off by rudeness, Mma," she whispered. "It is the rude person who is rude, not you."

This advice, puzzling at first, encouraged Mma Makutsi. "You are right," she whispered back. "I am not afraid of this woman. I am not afraid of a great big melon." She looked furtively at Mma Ramotswe, momentarily embarrassed by the childish nature of the insult. It was the sort of thing that Charlie would say, and not a fitting remark for the fiancée of the owner—virtually—of the Double Comfort Furniture Shop and an assistant private detective. But Mma Ramotswe had not heard, or had chosen not to hear.

The aunt glared at them as they came up to her. "You should not be here, Grace Makutsi," she said sharply, rising to her feet. "Did they not tell you that I would say when you could come? Did Gaethele not give you my message?"

She did not wait for an answer to her question, but continued, "And now you are bringing the whole world. This woman here, what business has she?" She gestured dismissively towards Mma Ramotswe. "Did anybody give you permission to bring her? This is not a cattle show, you know."

The sheer rudeness of this welcome made Mma Makutsi start; Mma Ramotswe felt it in her arm, a shocked movement.

"*Dumela,* Mma," said Mma Ramotswe quickly, extending the traditional greeting. "I hope you have slept well."

Even the aunt, in all her bristling hostility, could not overcome the ancient habit; she returned the greeting gruffly, but then immediately turned again to Mma Makutsi. "Well? Did Gaethele give you my message?"

Mma Ramotswe intercepted the question. "I think he did, Mma. But Mma Makutsi is the fiancée, you see, and I was the one who said to her that she should come to the hospital. I was the one."

The aunt stood quite still, absorbing this provocative piece of information. Then, without looking at Mma Ramotswe, she said to Mma Makutsi, "Who is this large person, Mma?"

"I am Precious Ramotswe," said Mma Ramotswe evenly. "Mma Makutsi works for me."

Mma Makutsi would have preferred it if Mma Ramotswe had said "works *with* me," but did not feel that this was the time for concern over status, important though such questions might be.

The aunt now looked at her adversary directly. Mma Makutsi was right, thought Mma Ramotswe; she does look like a melon. "So you are that woman," said the aunt. "I have heard of you and your detective nonsense. I do not want to think about such business now. The important thing is this: my Phuti is having a big operation. He is in there now. Now, now, while we speak. And I do not want him to see people until he is strong enough. That is all, Mma."

She stopped, and fixed Mma Ramotswe with the stare of one who has given a full and perfectly reasonable explanation.

"Have you spoken to the doctor?" asked Mma Ramotswe. She sounded neither angry nor offended; her tone was perfectly even.

"Yes, yes," snapped the aunt. "I have spoken to them and signed a piece of paper. They told me all about the operation that they would have to do. It is very sad."

Mma Makutsi caught her breath. "Why sad?"

"Any operation is sad," said Mma Ramotswe hurriedly. "It is sad for the person having an operation. Sad for the system. That is well known."

The aunt raised an eyebrow. There was something triumphant in her expression. "They gave me all the details," she said. "The doctor was very kind. He was Ghanaian. They are always kind, those people from that place."

Mma Ramotswe probed. "Maybe you could tell Mma Makutsi what he said. She is the fiancée, so she has the right to know."

The aunt moved her head slightly, as if to ease the pressure on her narrow shoulders. "Fiancée? What is a fiancée, Mma? A fiancée is not a *permanent* person; an aunt, an uncle, they are permanent. Forever. You see?"

Mma Ramotswe glanced at Mma Makutsi. Her assistant was looking down at the ground, avoiding the aunt's gaze.

"But she will be Mrs. Radiphuti," said Mma Ramotswe quietly. "She will be his wife very soon."

For a few moments there was complete silence. The conversation had been followed by the woman and the girl on the bench; understood by the woman, incomprehensible to the girl. The dog had opened its eyes when they had arrived, but had closed them again. A small cluster of flies had gathered at its nostrils, but it seemed inured to their presence.

Then the aunt spoke. "Not now," she said. "Not any more, I think."

Mma Makutsi's head jerked up. Mma Ramotswe's grip on her arm tightened.

"Yes," said the aunt, her eyes revealing her evident enjoyment. "Phuti will not wish to marry you now, I'm afraid. Not after this operation."

Mma Ramotswe drew in her breath; it was involuntary, but quite audible. She understood that it was his legs that had been damaged; what was this?

"The doctor told me," said the aunt. "He told me that Phuti's right leg is very badly damaged. All crushed, he said, like the wood you break up to make a fire. They cannot repair it, and they are going to have to cut it off. There. Just below the knee."

Mma Makutsi closed her eyes, and for a moment Mma Ramotswe thought that she was going to collapse there where they were standing. She helped her to the bench. "Sit down, Mma. Just sit down."

The aunt's satisfaction in the situation seemed to be growing. She now became brisk and businesslike. "The doctor said that he thought that they would be able to make a good flap of skin. They will not have to take skin from anywhere else. That is good. And then he will have to come to my house, and I will look after him." She paused. "I do not think that marriage will be a good idea now, Mma. And anyway, you will not want to marry a man who has only one leg, will you? You will find another man—there are plenty of men with two legs."

As Mma Makutsi settled herself on the bench, the woman at the other end moved over to her side, quickly, instinctively. "Do not be sad, my sister," she said. "You must not be sad. Your husband will not die."

Mma Makutsi looked at the woman, who now took her hand

in hers. "It does not matter that they will take one leg from him. It does not matter. He will be alive, won't he?"

Mma Makutsi nodded. "Thank you, Mma."

"And this lady," whispered the woman. "She is like a skinny cow. No man will want to live with her. Even a man with one leg will run away from such a woman. You can tell that."

Mma Ramotswe cleared her throat. "I have heard what you said," she told the aunt. "And I do not think you should speak like that. It is not true, and it is unkind. Mma Makutsi will wait here with me, and with this good lady here." She gestured to the other woman on the bench, who nodded her agreement. "And then when the operation is over she will go to sit with Phuti until he wakes up. I shall explain all this to Dr. Gulubane, who is an important doctor in the hospital here. I know him well, Mma, and I am sure that he will sort everything out if you start to make trouble." She paused. "Do you understand what I have said to you?"

The aunt glanced about her. The mention of authority had unnerved her, and she was outnumbered; even the young girl was staring at her with undisguised hostility. She reached for a bag that she had placed beside the bench and began to walk away. "Phuti will be very cross when I tell him about this," she said over her shoulder. "I can tell you that."

Mma Ramotswe hesitated for a moment, and then she walked briskly after the retreating aunt. "Excuse me, Mma," she said.

The aunt ignored her.

"I know that you're feeling very sad," Mma Ramotswe persisted. "I know that you love Phuti very much, and this must be very hard for you."

The aunt's step faltered.

Mma Ramotswe reached out to touch the other woman's

arm. "And from what I have heard, he is very fond of you too. He is a good man."

The aunt stopped. Mma Ramotswe heard her breathing, a slightly raspy sound; to hear the breathing of others, such a vulnerable, intimate sound, was the most powerful reminder of their humanity—if one listened.

"You have heard that he is fond of me, Mma? You have heard that?"

Mma Ramotswe had not, but she reasoned that she could infer it from what Mma Makutsi said about Phuti's regular visits to the aunt's house; and from such information to a conclusion of fondness, and from that to a *report* of fondness, was not too large a step. To tell the strict truth was the best policy in general but not *always,* particularly when the happiness of an insecure and lonely, even if misguided, woman was at stake.

"Yes, I have heard it," she said. "And I think that you should think very carefully about what I am going to tell you, Mma."

The aunt was looking at Mma Ramotswe intently now. The watermelon-shaped head gave a small nod.

"Phuti is a good man," Mma Ramotswe went on. "I have already told you that. And there is something that we need to remember about good men. They have room in their hearts for more than one person, you know. So if Phuti has a wife . . ."

"She is his fiancée," muttered the aunt.

"But she will be his wife, and what I was trying to tell you is that I am sure that he will still be very fond of you and look after you when he is married."

The aunt looked doubtful. "How do you know this? How do you know what he will feel?"

"I know it because I know Mma Makutsi very well," she said. "I know that she is the sort of woman who will make sure that he does his duty. She will not allow him to forget about you."

The aunt stared at her. "You are sure of that?"

"Of course I am sure. We can ask her right now if you like."

The aunt looked back towards Mma Makutsi. "Why?"

"Because each of you has a heavy heart," said Mma Ramotswe. "And feeling angry makes a heart even heavier."

The aunt made a strange sound with her teeth: a sucking-in of air. Then she made her decision.

"I do not wish to talk to you any more, Mma. Thank you very much. Goodbye."

CHAPTER SIX

HOW TO LOVE YOUR
COUNTRY AGAIN

PHUTI RADIPHUTI'S OPERATION took place on a Friday morning. Mma Makutsi spent the latter part of the afternoon at his bedside before being ushered out by a nurse and making her way home by minibus. She felt physically exhausted but also, curiously, elated: this came from sheer relief at the fact that Phuti was still alive, and also from the emotion that she had felt when he had taken her hand and held it tightly. That, she felt, could only be a wordless affirmation of the fact that nothing had changed.

"A word of warning," said the doctor as he took Mma Makutsi aside. "He won't necessarily have taken in what has happened to him. Sometimes it's not until quite a bit later that a person in his position comes to terms with the loss of a limb. You have to be ready for that."

This warning, sobering though it was, had not succeeded in dampening Mma Makutsi's pleasure at the operation's success. She had seized upon such positive words as the doctor had uttered: there had been enough skin for a very good flap; the compromised tissue was relatively low down the leg—just a couple of handbreadths above the ankle; a temporary prosthetic device could be fitted in a month or so and then they could get just the right artificial leg later on; his vascular system was fundamentally healthy, and there should be no reason why there should be any complications. There was a lot to be relieved about.

Later on that night, though, in the quiet, sleepless hours, doubts returned. The aunt had implied that everything would be different now that Phuti had lost a leg—but why? The posing of the question brought a range of possible answers. Phuti had never been particularly confident. This might destroy his confidence altogether, and if that happened then he might not wish to marry. He might become depressed, as Mr. J.L.B. Matekoni had been, and Mma Makutsi knew what depression could do to a person's ability to make even the smallest decision, let alone a decision about a wedding date. And finally there was the aunt with the watermelon-shaped head; she had now shown her hand, and could be counted on to use all her wiles—and Mma Makutsi imagined that these might be considerable—to prise Phuti away from her and take him back into the fold of his family. There were all sorts of unpleasant possibilities, and in the small hours of the morning these loomed larger and larger.

By Saturday morning, Mma Ramotswe had heard of the operation's success. She too had been going over various possibilities; in particular she had been thinking of the threat posed by the aunt. Mma Ramotswe had gone out of her way to reassure her, but when the other woman had simply brushed her off she realised that this was one of those people with whom there simply could be no dealing. They were few and far between, thankfully, but when you encountered one of them it was best just to recognise what you were up against, rather than to hope for some miraculous change of mind, some Road to Damascus improvement.

At least Phuti was alive and well, by all reports firmly embarked on the road to recovery, and Mma Ramotswe could get on with the day's activities without too much brooding and anxiety. Saturday was her favourite day of the week, and usually followed the same set pattern. There would be shopping to do at the Riverside Pick and Pay, one of the highlights of the week with important decisions to be made about vegetables and cuts of meat. The children liked to accompany her on these outings; she had to watch them carefully, or the shopping trolley would be filled with garishly packaged boiled sweets and chocolate, all carefully tucked under healthier produce.

"If you really want your teeth to drop out," Mma Ramotswe scolded, "then buy lots of those things. But if you still want to be able to chew anything when you're thirty, don't."

She realised, though, that such a threat meant nothing to them, particularly to Puso, for whom the idea of being thirty was inconceivable. Motholeli was a bit more prudent—she had seen how a world could draw in—but her younger brother, not yet ten, felt himself immortal. That would change, of course, but traces of that attitude, she thought, lasted well into adult life, and had to. The realisation of our mortality came slowly, in dribs and drabs, until we bleakly acknowledged that everything was on loan to us for a short time—the world, our possessions, the people we knew and loved. But we could not spend our time dwelling on our mortality; we still had to behave as if the worst would not happen, for otherwise we would not do very much, we would be defeated and give up.

That Saturday the children would not be going to the supermarket, as they had things to do with friends. Motholeli was going with her Girl Guide group to Mokolodi, for a nature talk from Mma Ramotswe's friend Neil Whitson, and Puso was accompanying a friend and his parents to their farm. So Mma

Ramotswe did her shopping by herself, hesitating by the sweet-biscuit shelves and surrendering to temptation; succumbing further at the bakery section, where she purchased a dozen sugar-dusted doughnuts; and exposing a final weakness on the way out when she paused at the newspaper counter and bought two expensive packets of ostrich biltong.

Her next call was the President Hotel, in the centre of town, where she sat at her normal table, the one on the left-hand side of the veranda, looking out over the open square below. The waiter, who knew her well, brought over a pot of red bush tea unasked, and a large fruit scone. She sat back in her chair and contemplated both with satisfaction. The world was an imperfect place— as the events of the last few days had demonstrated—but within that vale of tears there were many sites and times of quietude and contentment, and this place and this moment on the veranda was one such.

She looked out over the square, twenty feet or so below the raised veranda of the hotel. It was a typical bustling Saturday-morning scene, with shoppers and strollers moving lazily between the various traders who had their wares spread out on ground-sheets and on pieces of newspaper about them. A display of cheap sunglasses, examined with admiration by two young men and a woman in an unflattering yellow trouser suit; a stout woman selling dresses from a mobile rack; a cobbler conjuring sandals out of strips of rough leather—Mma Ramotswe marvelled at the ingenuity of the sellers in making attractive displays out of cheap merchandise. That is how we live, she thought, by selling things to one another, or by working, as she did, to make money to buy things from these people who were so keen to sell them. Not all the things we bought we needed; very few of them, perhaps, especially when it came to fancy shoes and dresses. How many outfits did you really need? she wondered. On the other hand, when you saw something you liked, then it so often seemed that you needed it, and in a sense, if you believed that you needed something, then you really did. She sighed. This was economics, and try as she might, she had been unable to make much sense of economics beyond the simple truism, so often stressed by her father, the late Obed Ramotswe, that one should not spend more money than one actually had. And yet, when one read the newspapers, that is exactly what so many economists seemed to recommend that people do. It was all very puzzling.

The fruit scone disappeared rather more quickly than she would have liked. The red bush tea, though, lasted: a single pot might be eked out over an hour, giving ample time to absorb what was happening below in the square and to plan the rest of the day. A Saturday-afternoon sleep, perhaps; there was a great deal to be said for that, especially in hot weather, when nobody would wish to be out in the sun until at least four o'clock. Then, with the sun beginning to sink, it might be cool enough to venture out into the garden and inspect the plants. On particularly hot days—as today was proving to be—they could look so discouraged, as if every drop of moisture had been sucked out of them by the dry air. But they had their ways: the plants in her garden were native to Botswana, and knew about heat and dust and how to make the most of every drop of rain that came to them. These were the waxy-leaved plants of the Kalahari, the mopipi trees, the strange, spiky aloes that sent up their red flowers in fierce defiance of the creeping brown of drought and aridity.

"Mma?"

Her thoughts were interrupted by a woman who had appeared at her side.

"Are you Mma Ramotswe, Mma?"

Mma Ramotswe looked up at the other woman. The stranger was older than her, but only by a decade or so. She was of traditional build herself, but her figure was largely concealed by the folds of a generously cut shift dress made out of a flecked green fabric. It was like a tent, thought Mma Ramotswe—a camouflage tent of the sort that the Botswana Defence Force might use. But I do not sit in judgement on the dresses of others, she told herself, and a tent was a practical enough garment, if that is what one felt comfortable in.

"I am Mma Ramotswe," she said. "Would you like to sit down, Mma? There is probably enough tea in the pot if we get the waiter to fetch another cup."

"Oh, I cannot drink up all your tea, Mma," said the woman. "But I will sit down. I am Mma Felo."

Mma Ramotswe inclined her head. She had heard of the name; the Felos had a hotel somewhere, she thought, and quite a few cattle too. They were influential people. "I have heard of your name," she said. "There is a hotel . . ."

The woman nodded. "That is us. It is very hard work, though, Mma. Never buy a hotel, Mma Ramotswe, unless you like working day and night."

"I will not buy one," said Mma Ramotswe. "I already have a business."

"Yes," said Mma Felo. "The No. 1 Ladies' Detective Agency. I have driven past your place—and your husband's garage too."

Mma Ramotswe wondered where the conversation was going. It was not unusual for people to approach her like this, circumspectly, indirectly, before the request for help was made. Was Mma Felo about to do the same? Mma Ramotswe waited, and then she said, tentatively, "Is there anything I can do to help you, Mma?"

Mma Felo's reaction was unexpected. She seemed to find this very amusing. "Oh no, Mma! My goodness, I do not need to be seeing detectives! Certainly not!"

Mma Ramotswe smiled. "Well, you never know, Mma. Lots of people seem to need my help. I did not mean to give you a fright."

Mma Felo assured her that she had neither taken offence nor been frightened. "I do not want anything of you, Mma Ramotswe," she said. "No, I just thought that I would say hello."

"That is very kind, Mma."

Mma Felo nodded. "I try to be a kind person, Mma. I have a lot of money, you know, and I am always giving it away. This cause, that cause. A school needs something. Can you buy it, Mma? This person needs an operation over in South Africa and there is no money. Can you help with the bus fare, Mma? And so on. It is never-ending." She paused. "And of course there is our friend, Mma Potokwane. I know that you know her, Mma. She has spoken to me about you."

Mma Ramotswe now remembered that Mma Potokwane had also spoken to her about Mma Felo. She had said something about her kindness; so that was true, even if Mma Felo mentioned it herself.

"I often used to see you, Mma," went on Mma Felo. "You used to drive past our place, past the hotel. You had that small van. That small white van."

Mma Ramotswe lowered her eyes. It was still raw, that place in her memory. "I had such a van, Mma."

Mma Felo spoke gently. "Mma Potokwane told me about it. She said that you were very sad when the van was sold. She said that your husband made you do it."

Mma Ramotswe shook her head. "No, that's not really true, Mma. My husband is a mechanic, as you know, and he had been saying for a long time that the van was getting a little bit old. He was probably right. He didn't make me do it—it was just that we couldn't fix it. That was all. We sold it for scrap, for spare parts or something like that. It went up north."

"To my nephew," said Mma Felo. She looked at Mma Ramotswe. "He is very good with his hands, you know. He is one of those natural mechanics."

Mma Ramotswe smiled, in spite of the memory of her van, in spite of that pain. "I know about such people, Mma. I married one."

Mma Felo agreed. Her own car had been repaired by her nephew on more than one occasion, and he had fixed her fridge, and washing machine, and many other small things about the house. "Everything would fall to pieces without such people," she said. "The whole country would fall apart, bit by bit."

For a moment Mma Ramotswe imagined a Botswana without mechanics, without people like Mr. J.L.B. Matekoni and Mma Felo's nephew. Nothing would work, and it would be like living full-time at some remote cattle post, where there was only sky and bush and the sweet smell of the cattle; where water would have to be fetched from remote wells where the bucket-winding mechanisms would eventually fail; where the roads would disappear because there would be no tractors and no graders to repair them. There were places like that in Africa—places where the mechanics had gone, or had never been in the first place; where the wind blew in dusty eddies about decaying buildings and broken masonry and signs that had long since ceased to be intelligible; where people had simply given up, had worked hard, perhaps, and dreamed, and then just given up. That was not Botswana, of course, but one had to be watchful.

"You are right about that, Mma," she said. "We would miss people like that."

She thought for a moment. It would be terrible if all mechanics were to be lost, but it would be unbearable if one mechanic, in particular, were to go. But that was a morbid thought, and she put it out of her mind; she and Mr. J.L.B. Matekoni were intending to grow old together, not for some time yet, of course, but at some distant point in the future. They would go to a village somewhere—Mochudi, perhaps—and sit under a tree on two stools and watch the cattle walk past. She could do crochet, perhaps, making tablecloths for other women to sell outside the Sun Hotel in Gaborone, and talk to grandchildren. Even if they would not be grandchildren by blood, the children of Motholeli and Puso would be grandchildren as far as she was concerned. They would play at her feet, and she would cook for them and sing to them the songs that she had forgotten at the moment but which she would learn again by the time she became a grandmother. Yes, that was an intriguing idea. Modern people had forgotten the old songs—the songs that the grandmothers of Botswana used to know; she could set up a course to teach them those songs again so that they could sing them to their grandchildren when they came along. *Mma Ramotswe's Refresher Course in the Old Botswana Culture;* that's what it could be called. Or they could call it *How to Love Your Country Again.* And Mma Makutsi could be an instructor too, in the old typing skills, perhaps, keeping alive the memory of typewriters when people had thrown them out in favour of computers. And shorthand, a skill that her assistant said was being learned by fewer and fewer people, even at the Botswana Secretarial College itself; she was sure that Mma Makutsi would not want that to be lost.

THAT WAS SATURDAY. On Sunday she went to the Anglican cathedral with the children, leaving Mr. J.L.B. Matekoni lying in bed, enjoying his one long sleep of the week. When she returned

she would make him his Sunday breakfast, which consisted of
boerewors and eggs and wedges of bread. "A man's breakfast," he
would say, smiling. And Mma Ramotswe would nod in agreement, but with the unexpressed mental reservation that there
were plenty of traditionally built women who would relish a
breakfast exactly like that, if it were not for the guilt they would
feel afterwards.

Puso went off with the younger children to the Sunday
school run in the general-purpose room of the cathedral; Motholeli, too old to be taught with the younger ones, had been
enrolled as a helper. She helped to hand out the books, and to
assist the small children in drawing their pictures of biblical stories. "No," she said, "the sea in this story is not coloured blue.
That is ordinary sea. This is the Red Sea." And a red crayon would
be selected and used to give a vivid shade to the parted waves,
tiny hands fumbling with the strokes.

In the place that she always occupied, halfway down and at
the end of a pew, a good spot from which to observe, Mma Ramotswe cast an eye over the congregation. There were no surprises,
although she did not recognise one couple sitting towards the
back, the man heavy-jowled, the woman wearing a blue hat and
a shawl in a clashing pink colour—not a good combination,
thought Mma Ramotswe, even if well intentioned. The Mma
Makutsi School of Fashion, she thought wryly, and then immediately took back the uncharitable observation, remembering
where she was. But it was true: Mma Makutsi did not have good
colour sense, and should not wear spots. Mma Ramotswe had
been thinking for some years of saying something to her about
that, but it was difficult. You could not say, *A lady who has a*
blotchy skin, Mma, should not wear spotted blouses. You could not.
And even if you were more tactful, saying something like, *Spots*
are nice, Mma, but I think that in your case stripes might be better,

there would still be the chance that the person to whom the advice was offered might ask why. Then, if you were truthful, you would have to explain. If you were truthful . . .

Mma Ramotswe did not believe in lying, but she did believe that there were occasions when one had to say things that were not completely true. We all do that, she thought, looking up at the cathedral roof: we all have to say things that are not strictly true in order to protect others from hurt. So she had to tell Mma Makutsi that she thought Phuti Radiphuti handsome, even when others would not; that, of course, had been in response to a direct question from her assistant, who suddenly said to her one morning, "Don't you think that Phuti is a very handsome man, Mma?" What could she do? So she said, "Of course he is, Mma; he is so kind too." The remark about his kindness was completely true, but that was not what Mma Makutsi was talking about, and she persisted. "Yes, he's very kind, Mma Ramotswe, but he is also very handsome. It is unusual, I think, to find people who are both handsome and kind. Don't you agree?"

Mma Ramotswe had been slightly irritated by this line of questioning. What about Mr. J.L.B. Matekoni? she might have asked. What about him? Phuti was not the only kind man in Botswana; Mr. J.L.B. Matekoni was widely known for his generosity, and was often taken advantage of for precisely that reason. Mma Potokwane, for instance, was always asking him to fix things at the orphan farm—old vehicles, a tractor, the boilers, the water pump—the list seemed endless. And so too was the list of Mr. J.L.B. Matekoni's good works, done without complaint or thought of reward, but noted, she believed, by everybody. Perhaps she should start writing a list in a book: *The Good Works of Mr. J.L.B. Matekoni;* it was not an entirely fanciful idea, as she could give it to the children later on, when they were older, and they could remember what a fine man their foster father was. She

wished that she had such a memento of her own father, the late
Obed Ramotswe—a scrapbook, perhaps, with photographs and
observations by people who knew him. But there was nothing like
that; just memories, of a man looking at her and smiling in the
way he did; of a voice that was gravelly and well used, but which
contained all that wisdom, all that experience, of people, of cattle, of a country that he had loved so dearly. All that. All that.

People were standing up and had begun to sing. She had
been thinking, allowing her mind to wander, and had not noticed
that the choir had started to come in. She stood up and watched
them as they walked past: Mma Mopoti in good voice, as usual,
the head chorister and pillar of the Mothers' Union. Mma Ramotswe would have to phone her and reply to the invitation to
address the Mothers' Union meeting next month on "The Life of
a Private Detective in Botswana." The title had been suggested
by Mma Mopoti, who was widely known for her ability to recite
family genealogy, navigating the intricate byways of cousinage
that linked just about everyone with everyone else. Mma Ramotswe would accept the invitation; she had to, as Mma Mopoti had
pointed out to her that they were distant cousins "way, way back,"
and one could not say no to a distant cousin, no matter how far
back the link was.

The members of the choir took their seats and the service
began. Mma Ramotswe made an effort to follow the proceedings,
but there seemed to be so much to distract her, and she abandoned her attempt. This was evidently to be a morning for thinking; no harm in that, and she was not the only one, she suspected,
looking about her. And Mma Mopoti herself, sitting there with
the choir, had closed her eyes and seemed to be nodding off. She
looked off to her right; there was that kind Indian family from
Kerala, who had invited her to their daughter's wedding, along

with seven hundred other guests; they loved their weddings, those people—almost as much as the Batswana loved theirs.

Her gaze moved on, and she spotted Mma Mateleke and her husband sitting just a few rows away. She thought it was strange that she had not noticed them before, as she usually exchanged greetings with her friend when she came in. Mma Mateleke was looking down at her hands, rubbing at something—a patch of irritable skin, Mma Ramotswe thought. And of course she could work out where that came from: nurses and midwives had to put that strong antiseptic on their hands—it could hardly do their skin any good. She had met a nurse who had had to find another job for that reason—scrubbing up for the operating theatre had made her hands bleed. She had ended up working in a bank, and had done well, handling money, which did not hurt the skin, but was every bit as dangerous as anything else one might handle.

Mma Mateleke stopped rubbing at her hand and glanced at her husband. Mma Ramotswe watched. Rather to her surprise, she saw that it was not an affectionate look. So Mma Mateleke was cross with Herbert Mateleke—that was interesting. But why? Wives could be cross with their husbands for so many reasons, ranging from the big sins of husbands (drinking too much, becoming violent, looking at other women) to the small sins that men committed so casually (not helping in the house, leaving clothes on the floor, forgetting birthdays and anniversaries, talking about football all the time). Herbert Mateleke was a mild man, rather mousy in his manner; it was difficult to picture him committing any of the big sins. And yet, and yet . . . Mma Ramotswe had been in practice as a private detective long enough to know that it was often the mild and inoffensive men who behaved most outrageously. Herbert Mateleke might look mild, but he might be having an affair with some blowsy woman somewhere, somebody like Violet Sephotho. Now that was a thought: Herbert Mateleke and Violet Sephotho! No, it was impossible, and she should not even think such thoughts, especially in the cathedral, and especially when the visiting priest was about to speak.

She would try to listen; she really would.

"My brothers and my sisters," the visitor began, "we are seated here with those we know and those we do not know. But even those we do not know are not strangers. We are united with them in a community which is brought together by one thing, and that one thing is love. It is that love that we profess before one another here today, and it is that love which joins many millions of people throughout the world, wherever gatherings such as that which we attend today take place. That is a sea of love. It touches on the shores of all. There is no place where you cannot see it, even if for some, for the poor and the oppressed, it seems far away, in the distance.

"There are people who say that what we are doing here has no meaning. That it is superstition, that it is wishful thinking. Wishful thinking? It is not that; it is not. Is it wishful thinking to say to yourself and to others that we must love one another? Is it wishful thinking to say that we must forgive others, so that love might grow within our hearts? Is it wishful thinking to imagine that it is only through an effort to love others that a hard and unhappy world may be transformed into a world of kindness and compassion? I do not think that it is.

"There are many creeds and beliefs; there are many ways of leading your life; there are many roads to oneness with the world. But there are other ways, too, and these are all about us. There are those who worship money and success. There are those who do not care about the suffering of others, as long as they are all right. There are those who think that science and mastery of the physical world will bring us happiness and save us at the end of the day. I cannot agree with any of these. I do not think that science alone will deliver us from the consequences of our greed and our stupidity—it is science that has made the very things that are poisoning our world. I do not think that material success will necessarily make us happier—the faces of the rich tell us that; I do not think that a big car or a big house makes a big man. I think that the measure of whether a life has been a good one is how much love there has been in that life—love both given and received.

"This is a place of love, here where we are gathered together today. Our message is love, not fear, nor enmity, nor dismissal of others. It is just love. That is all."

Mma Ramotswe listened to each of these words, as did all the others present. She glanced along the pew: a man who worked in the diamond office sat quite still, his eyes fixed on the face of this visitor; another man sat with his eyes raised to the ceiling, his brow knitted in concentration and reflection; and a woman in the next row, immediately in front of Mma Ramotswe, a woman whom she recognised but knew little about, other than that she lived by herself near the Sanitas tea garden, this woman, moved by some private sorrow as much as by the words being spoken, cried almost silently, unobserved by others, apart from Mma Ramotswe, who stretched out her hand and laid it on her shoulder. *Do not cry, Mma,* she began to whisper, but changed her words even as she uttered them, and said quietly, *Yes, you can cry, Mma.* We should not tell people not to weep—we do it because of our sympathy for them—but we should really tell them that their tears are justified and entirely right.

CHAPTER SEVEN

A BAD STORY ABOUT A
BAD WOMAN

MMA RAMOTSWE had told Mma Makutsi that she could have compassionate leave. "As many days as you like, Mma," she said. "You must be there at the hospital. You must be at Phuti's bedside—that is where you should be."

Mma Makutsi had thanked her, but assured her that she would only take a day or two at the most. She was not one to take unscheduled leave, and had always insisted on coming to work, even when suffering from the colds or flu that a lesser employee would have seized upon as an excuse for staying at home. "I am paid for a month's work," she said, "and that is what I shall always do."

But this was an exceptional situation, and even Mma Makutsi accepted the need to be away. Phuti Radiphuti was making good progress: there was no sign of infection, the doctors said, and his wound was healing nicely. "He is always so pleased to see you, Mma," confided one of the nurses. "I can tell that you will make him better quickly. Some relatives—ow!—they make sick people even sicker."

"Really?"

"Yes, Mma, I'm telling you! I have looked after a patient who I am sure died because he could not face going back to his wife. She came in here and nagged and nagged him. It was his fault he was ill. It was his fault there was no money. She should never have married a man like him when she could have done much better. And so on, and so on. He said to me, *I am going to go now. I cannot face that woman any more.* And he did, Mma. Would you believe it? He went the next day."

"And was she sorry? That wife? Was she sorry that he was late?"

"Not at all, Mma. She wailed—all right, she wailed a bit—but then, ten minutes later, she said, *That lazy man. Look what he has done now! He has gone and died, and who is going to look after everything? Me! It is always me. Always. Oh, he is a selfish man to die.*"

Mma Makutsi had been shocked by this story, but flattered by the nurse's tribute. She had seen how cheerful Phuti looked when she came to see him; she had seen his expression when he talked about what they would do when he was discharged from hospital; how they would start to furnish his house afresh, ready for the wedding. And the wedding? When would that be? She hardly dared ask the question, but asked it anyway, and he said, "I shall have to learn to walk again before I can get married. I have to be able to walk on this new leg of mine before I can have a wedding."

She discreetly interrogated the nurse about artificial limbs. "Six months?" said the nurse. "It will probably hurt him at first, but then the stump will toughen up and he will be all right. I have seen patients running after a minibus one year after they have lost a leg." The nurse paused. "Don't worry, Mma, he will still be a man. I know about these things. You must not worry about that."

Mma Makutsi had glared at her disapprovingly. That was none of her business, and she should not be making comments about private matters of that sort. But she was glad nonetheless to know that Phuti had not had any other injuries that she had not heard about.

WITHOUT MMA MAKUTSI, the office seemed very quiet. The garage was busy, though, and the mechanical noises that came through the shared wall were reassuring and companionable. Every so often she heard the apprentices raising their voices over something or other—those young men loved to shout, she thought—it is always those with the fewest sensible things to say who make the loudest noise in saying them. But they were just young men, and no worse, she felt, than any other young men. Or perhaps they were—certainly Charlie was, even if Fanwell had shown some better qualities. But we were all young once, she said to herself, and foolish, and eager to show the world how much we knew, when we knew so little; she could not blame Charlie and Fanwell for that.

The business, of course, had to continue, even in the absence of Mma Makutsi. There were several outstanding matters needing attention, including the case of Mrs. Grant; Mma Makutsi had been doing the preliminary work on that, and the investigation would have to wait until she got back to the office. But now there was a new client, a Mr. Robert Kereleng, who had telephoned to make an appointment for that morning. She would have preferred to have had Mma Makutsi with her for this meeting, as she valued her assistant's comments on new clients— provided, of course, that these comments were delivered after the client had gone.

At ten o'clock, shortly before Mr. Kereleng was due to arrive, she made herself a cup of red bush tea, using, out of deference to the absent Mma Makutsi, the smaller of the two teapots. Then she sat at her desk and waited until Mr. Polopetsi put his head round the door and announced that there was somebody to see her.

"I am free to help you," he whispered. "There is nothing for me to do in the garage—or nothing urgent—and since she is not here . . ." He looked longingly at Mma Makutsi's desk; he would have given anything to have occupied that desk, to be a full-blown assistant detective, but Mma Ramotswe had explained to him that there simply was not enough work and this was, after all, the No. 1 *Ladies'* Detective Agency. "It is not that a man cannot be a detective, Rra," she said. "It is not that. It is more a question of what the clients want. I think that they want to see lady detectives. That is just the way it is."

But with Mma Makutsi away, there was no reason why Mr. Polopetsi should not sit there. And his perspective on things—which was often rather astute—would be welcome.

"Of course you can sit in, Rra. That seat over there. But first, show in this Mr. Kereleng."

She tidied her desk, moving her cup to one side. That was another aspect of Mma Makutsi's absence—who would make the tea when the client came in? She had used the smaller teapot, and had made only enough for one. She could not ask Mr. Polopetsi; he knew how to make tea, but his drop in status—from assistant hospital pharmacist to unqualified garage hand and occasional sub-assistant detective (as Mma Makutsi put it)—was bad enough without rubbing it all in by making him into a junior tea-maker too. So there would just have to be no tea.

Mr. Kereleng was ushered in, and Mma Ramotswe saw a man in his early thirties, well dressed, and with a pleasant, open expression. She felt comfortable with him immediately, even before he greeted her in the polite, formal fashion, and shook hands firmly and sincerely.

"You are very kind to see me, Mma Ramotswe," he said.

"That is why we are here, Rra. We are here to see people."

He nodded. "I never thought that I would be coming to somebody like you," he said, and then, apparently embarrassed, he corrected himself. "Not that there is anything wrong with you, Mma. No, it's just that I never thought that I would need a detective."

Mma Ramotswe laughed. "Nobody does," she said. "People think that private detectives are for other people, and then they discover that there is something in their life that needs help, and that is when they turn to us. That is why we are here."

"Exactly," muttered Mr. Polopetsi. "Mma Ramotswe is the lady to sort out your problems."

Mr. Kereleng absorbed this.

"And what are these problems, Rra?" asked Mma Ramotswe.

Mr. Kereleng did not hesitate. "It is a woman," he said. "Let me tell you about it, Mma."

KERELENG. That is my name. Robert Monageng Kereleng, BSc. I don't always put the BSc in, Mma, but I tell you about it now because it is relevant to the story of my life. Do they do degrees in private detection, Mma? They don't? I was only joking. The University of Botswana has better things to do than to teach detection—sorry, Mma, that's not to suggest that what you do is not important. It is very important—and I mean that. Otherwise would I have come to see you?

"I have a BSc in biology. Yes! I knew when I was a very small boy—this high—that I wanted to be a biologist. I was always looking at how living things worked—trees, grass, seeds, frogs. Yes,

frogs! When I was a little boy—ten, maybe—I used to catch frogs
in the rainy season and cut them up to see how their organs
worked. I would not do that now, Mma, because if there is one
thing that biology teaches you it is to respect living things. Now I
would never kill anything unless it was for food. That is how much
I respect living things, Mma Ramotswe.

"Not even a snake. No, I would not. I would not kill a snake
unless it was necessary to do so to avoid being bitten. Snakes
have their role in the country's ecology, Mma, they have their
place. That is one thing that we really have to start teaching our
children. If you see a snake, do not pick up the first stone to
hand and throw it at the snake. Do not do that. That snake has
its purpose, even if it is a mamba or something like that. But that
is a very difficult lesson to teach people, you know, and I think
that there are some people who will not be content until there
are no snakes left in Botswana. Foolish people.

"We live in Gaborone, Mma. My father had a bottle store—
you may know the one, over by the supermarket. Yes, that one.
People used to call it a gold mine, and I wondered why they did
that when it was a store and not a mine. Then, when I got a bit
older, I knew that they were talking about how much money the
store made, which is true. My father made quite a bit of money.
Then he died. That is often the way it works, Mma Ramotswe:
a man makes a lot of money and then he dies before he has the
time to enjoy the fruits of his labour.

"My poor father would have liked to have enjoyed his money.
I said to him, 'Daddy, you are an old man now, and an old man
does not have to work. You have earned the right to sit in the sun
now. You are entitled to count your cattle.' He thought about this,
but he was worried about looking after the bottle store. 'You have
a good manager,' I said. 'He can run the store for you and you can

retire. That is the way to do it.' I did not want to run the bottle store, Mma, because I was studying biology and I wanted to work in a laboratory. You understand that, I think, Mma Ramotswe. I have heard people talking about you. They say that you are a lady who understands everything.

"My father listened to my advice. He was sad that I did not want to take over the bottle store, as it would have given him great pleasure to see a big sign above the store saying *Kereleng and Son*. But he wanted me to be happy and to do the things that I wanted to do, and so he put the manager in charge. 'He is a very good businessman,' he said to me. 'I shall not be surprised to find out after a year that I have not one bottle store, but two. Perhaps even three!'

"I said, 'I am very happy for you, my daddy. Now you can go back to the village and talk to all the old men there. You will have a lot to talk about after all these years.'

"He went back to the village, Mma Ramotswe, and I got a job in the Ministry of Agriculture, in their laboratory. I was very happy doing that work, and my father was very happy out in the village. He wrote to me every two weeks and told me what he and his friends were talking about. Which was not very much, Mma—you know how old men are. They always talk about the same things and tell the same stories many times. *Do you remember when we had that drought, the bad one? Do you remember that man who brewed the beer that made everybody sick? Do you remember . . .*

"He was very happy. But then, Mma, he became late. It was very sudden. He was talking with his friends and he just fell off his chair. It was a good way to leave, and he had had a good life. I was sad, of course, but I knew that he would have a good place in heaven, and that made it easier to bear. I was in charge of all his affairs, and went to see the manager of the bottle store. He yelled and wailed when I told him that my father was late. 'What is to happen now?' he cried. 'Oh, what is to happen?'

"I said to him, 'What do you mean—what is to happen? What do you mean?'

"He looked away. He would not meet my eyes. Then he said, 'Nothing. I did not mean to say that. It is just that when one is very sad all sorts of meaningless words come out. I did not mean to say anything but that I am sad. I am very sad, Rra.'

"I thought no more about it, but when I went round to the bottle store a few days later, I found that it was closed. There was a woman hanging about, Mma, and I recognised that she was one of the people who worked in the store. I said to her, 'What is happening here?' And she said, 'The manager has run away. There are some people over there who say that he is in Mahalapye now. I am waiting for my wages. Please pay me.'

"I am afraid that the manager had stolen most of the takings, Mma. For six months or more he had been taking money out of the till. When my father became late he feared that there would be people who would come and look at the accounts—lawyers and accountants—and so he ran away. I was left with some money, as the store itself was worth quite a lot, but it was not nearly as much as I would have got had the manager not been a thief."

MR. KERELENG sat back in his chair.

"So now you want me to find this manager of yours," said Mma Ramotswe. "Have you been to the police?"

Mr. Kereleng looked surprised. "No, I do not expect you to find him," he said. "You see, that was only Part One of my story. There is another part, which is called Part Two."

"Excuse me, Rra," said Mr. Polopetsi. "Would you like some tea? This is a very long story, and you might like some tea to drink while you are telling it to us."

Mr. Kereleng said that he would like tea, and for her part Mma Ramotswe was pleased that Mr. Polopetsi had offered to make it. It was interesting, she thought; some men are *more modern* than you think they are.

I WAS ANGRY with the manager, as you can expect, and I did try to find him. However I soon realised that there was very little I could do, as he had gone over the border to South Africa. Once people do that, Mma, then they are lost. If you are chasing anybody, catch them before they get to the border or you will never catch them. You may as well chase smoke rising from a fire.

"I put the money I had left into the bank, as I thought that I would buy a house. Then I could settle down and find a wife and start a family. It would be a very good life. But the way it worked out was the other way round—I found a lady first, before I found the house.

"Let me tell you about this lady. She is a very beautiful lady— one of the most beautiful ladies in Botswana. And it is not just me who says that—it is everybody. Anybody who meets that lady says the same thing. She could be Miss Botswana twice over, if you ask me.

"I met her at a hotel. There was a jazz concert, and I was there with some friends. This lady and some of her friends joined us—we had a very good time. She knew who I was, I think, because she had heard about our bottle store, as everybody had. I told her that I had sold the bottle store. She was interested in that. She asked me where I had put the money—only joking, she said. But I told her anyway—I said that I had put it in the Standard Bank. She laughed and said that the bank was always the safest place to put money, and that people who put their money under their beds were asking for trouble. She said that an aunt of hers had put two thousand pula under her mattress and had left it there for a year. When she went back, she discovered that the money had been eaten by ants, and there were only a few scraps of paper left.

"I saw this lady the following day, and we went for a drink in a different hotel. Then the next day we went to have a meal at the Sun Hotel. She liked that place, as she said it was very sophisticated. I said to her, 'Anywhere you like, I like.' And she said, 'We are very well suited—maybe we can live together. You did say that you were thinking of buying a house.' I told her that I was, and she suggested that we go and look for a house together. I could not believe my luck: here I was, going off to choose a house with one of the most glamorous ladies in Botswana, and I a scientific officer (second class) in the government laboratories. I thought that I was a very lucky man.

"We went to an agent. He showed us a house that was very bad—it had no bath, and there was a big stain on the kitchen floor. He said that he could not see this stain, but it was certainly there, as if a cow had been slaughtered right there. The next house, though, was better, and we both liked it. It was for sale at a very good price because the owner had gone to live in Francistown and needed to get rid of it quickly. I managed to knock another ten thousand pula off the price, and that was it. I had a house.

"This lady was very pleased. She was making me feel very proud and happy and when she said, 'It would be safer to put the house in my name,' I did not bother to ask why. I had read that this is what people sometimes did—they put the house in their wife's name so that if the bank came chasing after them they would not be able to take the house away. I went to see an attorney and we had everything fixed up. We were very pleased. 'We can have many children now,' said this lady, 'because we have somewhere to put them all.'

"I was such a happy man, Mma. I walked on my toes and my head was held high—like this. I started to talk to my friend about wedding dates. She said, 'All in good time. There will be plenty of time for these details once we have moved in and have started to be happy in our new house.'

"Oh, Mma, I can see that you can tell what is coming. And you are right. You are very right. We stayed in this house for two months, and then she invited her mother to come and stay with her. That was bad enough, but then she invited two aunts to live with us as well. I said, 'Where are we going to put all the children, with all these aunties about the place talking all day and making a big noise?' She said, 'They are my aunties, and a man who cannot accept the aunties of his wife had better not get married after all.' That was when I realised that she had never wanted to marry me, that she did not even like me, and that the whole thing was a trick to get the house out of me.

"I shouted at her and I threatened to call the police. She said, 'And what crime will you report to the police? Will you tell them that you have changed your mind about a present you gave to a lady? They will say, *What crime is that, Rra? You tell us.*'

"I went to see the attorney I had used to buy the house. He said to me that as far as he could make out, I had given the house to this lady and that there was nothing I could do about it. So I went back to the place I was staying in before—the house of an uncle of mine, who had allowed me to stay there as a lodger. Now I had no money left—just my salary. The manager of the bottle store had stolen most of my inheritance and this lady had taken what was left. I was very sad. I need to sell the house, you see, as I have been offered the chance to buy a small agricultural laboratory—it is my big chance. Then somebody said to me, 'You should go and see this Mma Ramotswe of the No. 1 Ladies' Detective Agency. If there is one person in Botswana who can help you, then it is her.' That is what they said, Mma, and that is why I am here."

Mr. Kereleng stopped. His hands folded in his lap, he looked down at the floor. Mma Ramotswe watched him; he was utterly dejected. She wanted to reach out and take his hand, but she could not do that with every client who came with a story of misfortune. She wanted to cry for him, but she could not do that either. There were not enough tears to shed for every story she heard of human foolishness and the unhappiness it brought in its wake.

So she simply said, "I am very sorry to hear this story, Rra. I am truly sorry."

"I am sorry too," said Mr. Polopetsi from the other desk. "It is sad to hear that there are such wicked women in Botswana."

Mma Ramotswe cleared her throat. "I am not sure what I can do for you, Rra. I shall have to think about what you have told me and see if I can come up with a suggestion. But it sounds as if the lawyer was right—you have given something away, and it is usually impossible to get a gift back once it has been made."

Mr. Kereleng sighed. "That is what everybody says, Mma. I thought that maybe you . . ."

"I shall see if I can think of something," said Mma Ramotswe. "It's just that sometimes I have to warn people right at the beginning that their case sounds very difficult, and that it may not be possible to help them. That is all."

"I understand," said Mr. Kereleng, his voice filled with defeat. "Thank you, Mma."

Mma Ramotswe moved the papers on her desk. She picked

up a pencil. "I need a bit of information," she said, sounding more businesslike. "You should give me the name of this lady and the address of the house."

Mr. Kereleng looked up. He was weary, with the look of one who knows that his case is no case. "She is called Violet," he said. "Violet Sephotho."

CHAPTER EIGHT

THE LADY OF THE AFTERNOON

MMA RAMOTSWE was as capable as anyone else of containing herself, but there were some situations—and this was one of them—where nobody could be expected to resist the urge to speak about something. After the departure of the unfortunate Mr. Kereleng, she and Mr. Polopetsi sat for almost half an hour discussing this latest story of Violet Sephotho's perfidious behaviour. Both were quite shocked; they knew of Violet's treacherous fiancé-stealing plans; they knew of her utter ruthlessness when it came to any men, fiancés or others; but now she was revealed as a downright thief and trickster, and that was something new.

It was all very well talking to Mr. Polopetsi about it. He knew all about Violet and disapproved of her strongly, but talking to a man about something like this, although satisfying, was not quite as good as a discussion with another woman, and with Mma Makutsi in particular. She had been Violet's victim on more than one occasion, and would naturally be most interested to hear all about this new instance of her rival's wickedness.

Mma Ramotswe had not intended to bother her assistant

during her compassionate leave, but by four o'clock that after-noon she could no longer bear to leave the news unconveyed.

"I am going to check up on Mma Makutsi," she announced to Mr. J.L.B. Matekoni in the garage workshop. "I am closing the agency for the day."

Charlie, who was leaning against the side of a car wiping a car part with an oily rag, looked up.

"Are you going to check up that she is not having a party?" he asked. "You know her, Mma. Compassionate leave? Passionate leave!"

"Do not say such things," snapped Mr. J.L.B. Matekoni.

"That was not very kind, Charlie," said Mma Ramotswe.

Charlie looked wounded. "I was only joking, Mma! Just a joke!"

"Can you see Mma Ramotswe or me laughing?" asked Mr. J.L.B. Matekoni. "Are we laughing at your joke?" He turned to Mma Ramotswe. "Tell her that I hope that Phuti is doing well and will be back on his feet soon."

"He has only got one foot now," muttered Charlie.

"What was that, Charlie?" said Mr. J.L.B. Matekoni. "Did you say something?"

"Charlie is only trying to be helpful," said Mma Ramotswe, giving the apprentice a sideways look. "And remember this, Char-lie: there but for the grace of God go you. Remember that."

She got into her van—the new blue van that drove so smoothly—and made her way over to Mma Makutsi's house. It was possible that she was at the hospital, she thought, but if she had been there in the morning—as she said she would be—then she might be home by now. And turning into Mma Makutsi's street, a street of modest houses occupied, she imagined, by people for whom reaching even this level of prosperity and comfort had been a battle, she pictured Mma Makutsi's reaction to this piece of news about Violet. It was an odd thing, thought Mma Ramotswe, that we take such pleasure in hearing news of some piece of bad behaviour on the part of one of whom we have come to disapprove. Such news should sadden us, as any news of human failings should do, but it tended to do the opposite. Why? Because it confirmed the view we had of such people, and laid to rest doubts about our judgement. *So, you see, I was right about her!*

Which is more or less what Mma Makutsi said when Mma Ramotswe found her at home. "I am not surprised at all," said Mma Makutsi. "I have always said that she was a bad woman, right from the first time I saw her at the beginning of our course at the Botswana Secretarial College. You should have seen her, Mma, looking out of the window with such an expression of boredom on her face. Why go to a secretarial college if you are not going to pay attention to what is being taught you? Why bother? Why not just go straight to one of those bars and become a lady of the afternoon?"

"Lady of the night," corrected Mma Ramotswe gently. "Mind you, we have no proof that Violet was ever involved in that sort of thing. We must be fair to her."

"Fair to her!" exclaimed Mma Makutsi. "Was she being fair to me when she got a job at Phuti's shop for the only reason that she wanted to take him away from me? Was that fair, Mma?"

Mma Ramotswe made a calming gesture. "Maybe not. All I am saying is that we should not accuse her of things that she has not done. As far as we know, she has never been one of those girls who sit about in bars."

"But you yourself said that this Mr. Kereleng person met her in a bar. Did he not tell you that? What was she doing in the bar in the first place, Mma? That's what I want to know."

Mma Ramotswe felt that there was little point in further discussion of this aspect of the matter. "Whatever else she may have done, Mma, the issue is this: How do we help this poor man? Have you any ideas?"

Mma Makutsi thought for a moment. "He is a very foolish man," she said. "Imagine putting your house in somebody else's name, especially when that somebody is Violet Sephotho! How stupid can you be!"

It seemed to Mma Ramotswe that this did not help. Mma Makutsi may not be herself after all the strain of Phuti's accident and operation, but she should know by now that this was not how one spoke of one's clients, most of whom were vulnerable in some way, or afraid. "Whether or not he was stupid," she began, "that is . . ."

"Very stupid," said Mma Makutsi. "Not just ordinary stupid—very stupid."

Mma Ramotswe sighed. "Maybe. But what about my question, Mma? Can you think of any way of helping this man?"

"No," said Mma Makutsi quickly. "I do not see what we can do. I have no ideas at all. None."

"So Violet Sephotho will get away with it?"

Mma Makutsi grimaced. "That is a very bad thought, I admit. But I'm afraid, Mma, that you are right. Sometimes wickedness prevails."

Sometimes wickedness prevails. The succinct words echoed in Mma Ramotswe's ears. It was probably true—there were times when wickedness seemed to be so firmly entrenched that any attempt to dislodge it, any rebellion against it, appeared futile. That had happened; many people had led their whole lives under the shadow of wickedness in its manifold guises—under oppression or injustice, under the rule of some grubby tyranny. And yet people often managed to overcome the things that held them down because they refused to believe that they could not do anything about it, and acted as if they could do something. It had happened before and it would happen again. In her short career as a private detective, Mma Ramotswe had encountered relatively few instances of evil, but she had seen some, and in each case she had seen the wings of wickedness clipped. Violet Sephotho had now stepped over a boundary that separated mere nastiness from real wickedness. She could not be allowed to prevail; she could not, and Mma Ramotswe told Mma Makutsi as much. But Mma Makutsi still doubted if anything could be done; although she now conceded that she would at least try to think of something, she held out little hope of coming up with a solution.

That issue put aside, they went on to talk of Phuti. "He is going to be discharged in a few days," said Mma Makutsi. "The doctor says that he has rarely seen an amputation that went so well."

The gist of this message was positive, but the word *amputation* hung in the air between them. There was an awful finality about it; an amputation might be treatment, but it had a ring of desperation to it, a sense of last resort.

Mma Makutsi went on bravely. "They have already measured him for a temporary leg," she said.

"That is good," said Mma Ramotswe. "Then he will get a permanent leg later on?"

Mma Makutsi nodded. "I think that is the plan. Temporary leg, then permanent leg."

"I am very sorry about all this," said Mma Ramotswe. "You know that, don't you, Mma? You and Phuti did not deserve this thing. You have been so good to him, and he is such a fine man. But we cannot control the things that happen, can we?"

Mma Makutsi considered this. "We cannot. And thank you,

Mma, for saying that you are sorry. That makes my heart feel a little bit better."

They drank tea together. Then Mma Ramotswe left to return home. She was no longer worried about Mma Makutsi; her assistant, she was sure, had deep wells of strength and character to draw upon. If you came from Bobonong, if you came from nothing and nowhere and got to where she had got to, then you were capable of dealing with most forms of adversity; she was sure of that.

THE NEXT DAY, with Mma Makutsi still on compassionate leave, Mma Ramotswe decided to start work on the case of Mrs. Grant. It would be a good case, she thought—there were few duties in life that were more enjoyable than that of informing another person of some piece of good fortune. Occasionally it fell to her during the course of her work to do just that—to give somebody the news of an unexpected inheritance from a forgotten relative, or to tell them of an insurance payout, or even a reward. Individual reactions to this sort of news varied; there were those who were frankly ecstatic, who ululated with delight; others were more controlled and pensive about why this stroke of good luck had come to them; others were greedy, and eager to find out whether the money they were about to receive could in any way be increased. If there was one legacy, might there be another? Might the insurance company be persuaded to pay out just a little bit more? For the most part, though, people were simply human in such circumstances, and behaved like children to whom a large bag of sweets had suddenly been dispensed. And why not? For most people, life was hard, and either uneventful or composed of the wrong sort of event; these little moments of material pleasure were harmless enough in the grand scheme of things.

She knew how to break the news of Mrs. Grant's gift. She would tell the guide that his kindness was about to be rewarded. Then she would ask him what he would really like to do with an unexpected windfall. He would think of sensible things to do—people always did when asked that question—and then she would tell him that he would be able to do what he wanted. Finally, she would talk about the Standard Bank, and the various sorts of accounts that they offered to new customers. And with that, her duty would be done. It would be a simple, open-and-shut case, except for one thing, and she thought of it now as she prepared to leave the office and begin her inquiry. That thing was this: very few matters were simple—if they involved human beings, that is—and nothing, in her experience, was open-and-shut.

But the very beginning of an inquiry was not the time to entertain such doubts, and so she put them out of her mind. This stage of the case, at least, would be straightforward. She would go and speak to her friend Hansi, who ran a safari agency in town. He would be able to identify the safari camp in question on the basis of the one bit of information they had—the name involved a bird, or perhaps an animal. That done, she would get the name of the manager from him and after that a simple telephone call . . . She paused. The safari camp would be somewhere up near Maun, as most of them were, in the Okavango Delta. It was a part of the country with which she was not familiar, and she had been waiting for a chance to go there. And it would be better to find the guide in person, and be absolutely sure that he was the right man . . .

Then there was the question of Mma Makutsi. It was clear to

her that her assistant had been under considerable stress, which was, of course, entirely understandable; she could imagine how she would feel if it had been Mr. J.L.B. Matekoni who had been injured and who had lost part of a leg. And if she were in that position, then a trip to Maun would be exactly the sort of thing to lift her spirits. Yes, that was exactly what they both needed. She herself needed a short break—Mma Ramotswe never took a holiday—and Mma Makutsi needed something to take her mind off what had happened. Maun it would be.

By the time she had parked her van in the car park behind the President Hotel, and agreed with the young man who appeared at her window that he could look after it, she was already planning the trip in her mind. She would have to look at her wardrobe to decide what to wear—visitors who went up there all wore khaki, with many of the women, even those of traditional build, wearing khaki trousers equipped with multiple pockets. That was a mistake, thought Mma Ramotswe; women of traditional build were fortunate in having comfortable built-in seating arrangements, but that did not mean to say that they should draw attention to this fact by wearing trousers. The appropriate garment for the traditionally built woman was a long skirt, or a large dress, which could *flow* around her in a way that enhanced her traditional figure.

And Mma Ramotswe did not see herself in khaki, either. Not only was that not a colour for ladies, but it did not achieve the objective of disguising the wearer from wild animals. Lions and the like, she thought, were not so stupid as to think that people wearing khaki were not there; such creatures knew full well that people in khaki were just people dressed in brown, and therefore every bit as dangerous to the wild animals as people in blue or red or some other bright colour. And if one wanted to be camouflaged, then the best garb, surely, would be something in green, which might make one look like a tree, if one was a tall person, or a shrub if one was not so tall.

There were other things, apart from the issue of dress, that would have to be thought about before they left for Maun. There was the issue of where to stay: the camps themselves were for visitors, with prices that only visitors could afford; but this did not present a problem for local people, who would have recourse to the hospitality of relatives or at least friends, or possibly relatives of friends, or friends of relatives' friends. In Mma Ramotswe's case there was Mr. H.B.C. Matekoni, a cousin of Mr. J.L.B. Matekoni, who had stayed with them on his last visit to Gaborone—an eight-day stay, while he was attending a training programme for aircraft mechanics, which was what he was. Mma Ramotswe was not one to keep a tally when it came to favours, but his eight-day stay would surely entitle her and Mma Makutsi to beds for the two or three days that their mission would need. She had not met Mr. H.B.C. Matekoni's wife, who was a primary-school teacher in Maun, but she had heard good reports of her, and the cementing of family relationships was another good reason for making the trip.

She found Hansi in his travel and safari office, sitting at his desk, engaged in a telephone conversation that entailed frequent and expressive hand gestures. He cast his eyes upwards when she came in, implying to her that it was a difficult client on the line, and then he signalled for her to sit down.

"Yes, yes," he said into the phone. "Yes, I am not saying that you are not entitled to a refund. What I am saying is that the refund must come from the tour operator and not from this office. That is what I am saying."

There was an angry crackle from the other side, and the conversation came to an end. Hansi laid the receiver back in its cradle and looked apologetically at Mma Ramotswe. "Not my fault, Mma. I cannot guarantee that everybody sees a leopard. You know how secretive those creatures are, looking out at us from their hiding places and laughing . . ."

Mma Ramotswe smiled. "It is the same with me, Hansi. I have clients sometimes who think that I have guaranteed a miracle. They can be very difficult."

"Perhaps we should be in simpler jobs, Mma Ramotswe. Ones where we are the clients and can make complaining telephone calls to other people." He paused. "Not that I can ever see you complaining, Mma. You are too kind. Nobody would take your complaints seriously. They would say, *Oh, very funny, Mma Ramotswe! So you are very happy then. Thank you.*"

"I am not always kind," said Mma Ramotswe. "I can get cross, the same as everybody else."

Hansi looked doubtful. "I do not think so," he said. "But let us not talk about people like that person on the phone to me just then. It is very good to see you, Mma—is there any reason for this visit, or is it just time for tea?"

"I want to go to Maun," said Mma Ramotswe.

Hansi raised an eyebrow. "You, Mma? You want to go on a safari?"

"Of course not. But I need some information for a case I'm working on. I need to find out about somebody who works up there. A person whose name I do not know who works in a camp that also has a name I do not know."

Hansi listened. "If you do not know either of those things, I do not know how I can help."

She explained that there was a clue. "The name of the camp is something to do with a bird, or possibly an animal."

Hansi thought for a moment. "If it's a bird," he said, "then it must be Eagle Island. It's also called Xaba-Xaba, but people find difficulty saying *x*, and so they decided to call it Eagle Island. That must be the camp."

"That is all I need to know. That, and their telephone number."

"There isn't an ordinary telephone at the camp," said Hansi. "They have a satellite phone, I think, but they usually use the radio. But you can speak to their office in Maun. They can get in touch with them."

She asked about the camp, and he gave her further details. He had been there once himself, on a trip that the owners of the camp had organised for tour agents. "I have never been so comfortable in my life," he said. "Never. And they were very good to us."

"I have heard as much," said Mma Ramotswe. "There was a certain Mrs. Grant who also thought that."

"I met the manager," Hansi went on. "I am sure that he will help you in your inquiry, whatever it is. And I also know one of the guides there. He is a very good man. He is called Mighty, and he can look at the ground and tell you about all the animals that have passed that way since, oh, five days ago. He reads the ground like a book. If he saw your footprints he would say, *Lady of . . .*"

"Of traditional build," supplied Mma Ramotswe.

"Exactly. *Lady of traditional build. She went by here five hours ago. Heading north.*"

"They are very clever, those people, Hansi."

Hansi nodded. "Sometimes I worry, though. I worry about who will be learning those skills in the next generation. Are there apprentices? Are there people learning how to track?"

Mma Ramotswe frowned as she thought of the apprentices at Tlokweng Road Speedy Motors. She could not imagine Charlie and Fanwell tracking animals through the bush, although she could just see them tracking cars. *Four-door saloon, heading south, third gear.* Or, more likely, *Car full of girls, going that way, two hours ago.*

Hansi made tea, and they continued to chat for half an hour or so. They enjoyed each other's company, although their circumstances were very different. He came from the opposite end of the country, from Ghanzi, in the far west, on the other side of the Kalahari, a dry place that had just enough vegetation to make it good land for cattle, as long as they were grazed thinly enough on the brittle veld. It was a landscape of browns and ochres, of dust and copper-red sunsets, of rickety windmills turning above marginal boreholes, sucking the land for water somewhere deep down.

Hansi's father was one of a tribe of Afrikaaners that had trekked there in the nineteenth century and had stayed. They were tough people, burned dry by the sun, leather-hard in their determination to eke out a living from the land, followers of a Calvinist church, a long way from their Dutch roots—so long a way as to have become African in their souls. This father of his had produced Hansi by a local woman, a Motswana, and then disowned his tiny son, sending the woman away with a pittance. Hansi knew who he was, and knew his farm, but knew too that he was not welcome there. Yet he was, for some complex reason, proud of this farmer who denied him, and of his lineage, and spoke of his father with the same air of pride as Mma Ramotswe spoke of hers. She thought, though, If I could speak to that man and tell him how much his son loves him, and shake him until he acknowledged this love and how stupid he was to turn his heart against it. If I could speak to him . . . But some of us cannot see love, she said to herself, even when it is there, right before us, asking us to invite it in.

After her conversation with Hansi, Mma Ramotswe returned

to the office. There she found Mr. Polopetsi sitting in Mma
Makutsi's chair. "Just trying it, Mma Ramotswe," he said. "And it is
important to have somebody here to answer the telephone."

Mma Ramotswe smiled at the explanation. She understood:
Mr. Polopetsi would never get promotion as long as Mma Makutsi was there; it was understandable, then, that he might wish to
enjoy the *thought* of being in her position.

"The lady whose chair that is," she said, "is a very determined
lady. You know that, don't you, Rra?"

Mr. Polopetsi nodded ruefully. "She is a very strong lady."

"And I'm afraid that she is showing no signs of giving up her
job," Mma Ramotswe went on. "Which means . . ."

Mr. Polopetsi interrupted her. "I know, Mma. There is no
chance for me." He paused and looked up, hoping to read
encouragement in Mma Ramotswe's expression. "I just wondered
whether poor Radiphuti's accident will make any difference. I
thought that maybe with him being crippled now, she would need
to stay at home."

"I don't think that he would like you to say that he is crippled," said Mma Ramotswe. "He has lost a leg—or a bit of a leg—
but they will fix him up with something and he will be able to
walk. Maybe more or less the same as before."

Mr. Polopetsi said that he was pleased to hear this, and Mma
Ramotswe thought that he meant it, even if the implication of
this news was that Mma Makutsi would stay at her post. She
wished she could do more for this mild and inoffensive man, who
was always so willing to take on new tasks and who never com-
plained. A great wrong had been done him, she felt, in his impris-
onment for the consequences of an error that was not of his
making, and in the past she had entertained thoughts of clearing
his name. But no longer; it was too long ago and it would be an
impossible task. Now he should concentrate on forgetting that

nightmare, which she thought was exactly what he was doing. But it would still be a help to give him some scrap of status to hang on to . . .

"I've been thinking, Rra." She had not—not strictly so—as the thought had just popped into her mind a few seconds ago. "I've been thinking about your position."

He looked at her with that long, hopeful stare that he often used—rather like the mute gaze of a dog that wants his master to feed him.

"Yes," she went on, now thinking quickly. "You know that this is a small business. We do not make much money, and the share we put in of the wage that Mr. J.L.B. Matekoni pays you is very small. You know that?"

He inclined his head slightly. "I know that, Mma. And I am very grateful."

It was typical of him, she thought. Others would resent this arrangement, but he accepted it.

"So we cannot really give you more money. We would like to, but we cannot."

"I know that, Mma. And you must not worry. My wife is helping in a shop now, and she is getting some money too. We are luckier than many. I am not complaining."

Mma Ramotswe nodded. "You do not complain, Rra. You are very good that way. But what I've been thinking about is this. We could give you a new title. I thought that we might call you . . ." She hesitated. She had thought of Operations Manager, but she knew that Mma Makutsi would object to that. So it would have to be Consultant. That was the word people used to describe the jobs of those who really had no fixed role, and sometimes nothing at all to do. "How about Consultant Detective?" she asked.

Mr. Polopetsi said nothing.

"It is a very good title," Mma Ramotswe encouraged him.

He shook his head. "It is kind of you, Mma. But I am happy as I am. You do not have to find a name for me just to make me feel better."

"But . . ."

"No, Mma. I do not need that. I am happy to do the work I do. Maybe one day things will change for me, but I do not fret too much about that. I am happy right now. I like fixing cars, you see, and I like doing some work for you too. So what do I lack? I have enough food now. My children are not hungry. They are learning well at school. This is a good country, our Botswana. So why do I need to be a consultant?"

She could not answer, and so she simply looked at him, and he looked back at her. Everything was perfectly understood.

Then he said, "While you were out, there was a telephone call for you. I took it. It was that lady who is your friend, that Mma Mateleke. She said, *Could Mma Ramotswe meet me for tea tomorrow morning at ten o'clock? Riverwalk. That café she goes to.* I said that I would ask you and that I would phone her and let her know."

Mma Ramotswe wondered if her friend was in trouble. She had looked ill at ease in church on Sunday, and the thought had crossed her mind that something was troubling Mma Mateleke. Domestic disputes, perhaps? She remembered the story that Mr. J.L.B. Matekoni had told her—about rescuing Mma Mateleke's car from the Lobatse Road. He had said something about strange behaviour from some man who drove past, but he had not said much more than that, and she had been cooking at the time rather than listening. Was something going on in the Mateleke household? She would find out, no doubt, at the Riverwalk Café tomorrow morning at ten o'clock.

She stopped. Why was it called Riverwalk? Where was the river? The Notwane was nowhere in sight. And the walk?

CHAPTER NINE

RULE 32

I T WAS VERY FORTUNATE that when Mma Ramotswe arrived at the Riverwalk Café the next morning she was able to get the table that she wanted. This was in the middle, but also on the edge. This was the best place to be, she thought, because it afforded a good view of the car park as well as of the small market that sprang up each morning to sell brightly coloured garments, necklaces, and a seemingly endless supply of carved wooden hippos. Mma Ramotswe had wondered who bought these carvings, as the stalls never seemed to do any business when she was there; the occasional visitor, perhaps, who felt the need for a hippo; the traveller buying a last-minute present for those left at home—unnecessary purchases, perhaps, but tokens of love that were never unnecessary, never pointless. She had bought a wooden hippo herself one day, only a small one, on impulse, when she had walked past a stall and seen the look of resignation on the stallholder's face. It had not been expensive, and she had not attempted to bargain as the seller expected her to do, but had paid the price asked without demur. The stallholder had cheered up, and Mma Ramotswe had remarked that perhaps business might improve. "There is always somebody to buy something," she said. Yes, she thought, including a somebody who bought a wooden hippo for which she had no real use just because she was soft-hearted.

The hippo had lain in a drawer of her desk for several days. Each time she opened it, he had looked out at her through the tiny indentations that were his eyes, as if to reproach her for his waterless exile, and she had wondered what to do with him. She had shown it to Mma Makutsi one morning, and her assistant had looked at her in puzzlement.

"That is a hippo, Mma Ramotswe. You have a hippo."

It had been difficult to contradict. "Yes, it is a small hippo."

Mma Makutsi waited expectantly, but said nothing. Mma Ramotswe had hoped that an admiring remark would have been made; then she would have presented it to her. But no such remark was forthcoming.

"It's very skilfully carved," she said at last. "You can even see his eyes. See? Those little marks there—they are the hippo's eyes."

"They are made by machines," said Mma Makutsi.

"I do not think so, Mma. This is a work of art. There is a sculptor somewhere who makes these animals."

Mma Makutsi shook her head. It was a shake that she gave when she knew that she was on firm ground. "I do not think so, Mma. There is a machine with different buttons. If you press one, then you get a hippo like that. And then there is another button for an elephant, and a giraffe too. They are very clever, these machines."

Mma Ramotswe felt a growing irritation. Mma Makutsi could be very dogmatic, and had been known to defend an indefensible position long after she had been shown to be wrong. These were hand-carvings—they were not the product of some ridiculous machine. No machine could make these curves in wood; no machine could put the eyes in exactly the right place. It was impossible. "You've seen a picture of such a machine, Mma?" she asked.

"You do not need to see pictures of things to know about them," Mma Makutsi answered blandly.

It had been a pointless discussion, and she had replaced the hippo in the drawer. It was not her fault if Mma Makutsi could not appreciate art, and could not tell the difference between handmade and machine-made objects. Yet as she replaced the hippo, she sneaked a look under its belly. *Made in China* would have settled the argument in favour of Mma Makutsi, but there was no such label, and she was reassured.

Later that day she gave the hippo to Mr. J.L.B. Matekoni. "I have bought you a present," she said. "I spotted it at that market at Riverwalk."

He took the hippo in his hands and examined it carefully. "It is very beautiful," he said. "I am very happy with it. It will be a . . . a treasure."

"You'll see that even the eyes are just right," said Mma Ramotswe. "Look at how they have made the eyes."

Mr. J.L.B. Matekoni peered at the hippo. "Very accurate," he said. "I wonder if they have a machine to help them do that, Mma? Do you think so?"

Now, sitting at her table in the Riverwalk Café, waiting for her meeting with Mma Mateleke, she let her gaze wander over the nearest stall. There were no carved hippos—fortunately—but clothes: shirts, dresses, and aprons. A breeze caught one of the shirts and filled it with air for a few moments, and she watched it moving, writhing, as if it were worn by a ghost, now a sedately dancing ghost, now the ghost of an agitated contortionist.

She was watching the shirt when Mma Mateleke arrived.

She was late, she explained, because of a baby who had been unwilling to be born. "Sometimes," she said, "I think that there are some babies who know something about the world. They say, *I don't think I want to go out there!*"

Mma Ramotswe laughed. "Sometimes it is not easy to be born into this world."

"But would we prefer it to be otherwise?" asked Mma Mateleke, settling herself into her chair.

"No," said Mma Ramotswe. "We are very lucky to be alive."

For a moment Mma Mateleke, who had been smiling, hesitated, her smile fading.

Mma Ramotswe noticed. "You don't feel lucky to be alive just now?"

Mma Mateleke sighed. "It's better than not being alive, I suppose. But there are times when . . . well, there are times when . . ." She did not finish her sentence. The waitress had appeared and they gave their orders, Mma Mateleke having coffee and Mma Ramotswe red bush tea. The waitress scribbled down the order and went off. Mma Ramotswe looked at her friend.

"You're unhappy, Mma?"

Mma Mateleke did not answer immediately. She was seated directly opposite Mma Ramotswe, on the other side of the table, but her eyes were focused elsewhere, looking out into the distance, to the tops of the gum trees lining the road beyond the car park.

"I am happy sometimes, Mma. Then, at other times, I am not happy." She looked at Mma Ramotswe, as if searching for confirmation. "I think that is probably how it is for most people."

Mma Ramotswe nodded. "Yes," she agreed, "there are times when I am unhappy and times when I am happy. There are more happy times than unhappy ones, I think."

"Perhaps," said Mma Mateleke.

Mma Ramotswe waited for her to say something more, but the other woman was now looking down at the ground, and did not seem to be ready to add to what she had said. "I think that you are unhappy now," she said, adding, "even if at other times you are happy."

It was not a remark to take the discussion much further—Mma Ramotswe was aware of that—but it seemed to move something within Mma Mateleke. "Oh, Mma Ramotswe," she said, "I am very unhappy. I am very unhappy with my husband."

Mma Ramotswe reached out and laid a hand on her friend's arm. "So, Mma, that's what it is. It is the same thing that makes so many women unhappy." And it was; she knew that only too well in her profession. How many women had made their way into her office and started off the consultation with, *It is my husband, Mma*? How many? She had made no attempt to count them, although the answer could be obtained easily enough by looking through the file that Mma Makutsi kept entitled *Unfaithful Husbands*. In this file her assistant entered the details of every consultation, every investigation, of such a matter. "It is a very thick file," Mma Makutsi had once observed. "This is a file that any man should be ashamed to see."

Mma Ramotswe spoke gently. "He is not behaving well?"

Mma Mateleke shut her eyes. She shook her head slowly. She bit her lip.

"So," said Mma Ramotswe. "He is being unkind?"

This brought a shaking of the head. "No, Mma. He is a generous man. He always gives me as much money as I ask for. It is not that."

Mma Ramotswe hesitated. An accusation of adultery was a serious matter, even if made in the context of a private consultation, which this effectively was. "He is . . . He's involved with another woman?"

Mma Mateleke looked up. "You've heard that too, Mma?"

"No. I was asking you a question."

Mma Mateleke looked disappointed, or so Mma Ramotswe thought, although she quickly realised that she must have misread her friend's expression; a wife does not wish to hear news of her husband's unfaithfulness.

"I think he's having an affair," said Mma Mateleke. "I think there is another woman somewhere. Some younger woman. Some younger, glamorous woman."

"Do you know who she is?" asked Mma Ramotswe. Violet Sephotho? She had briefly entertained such a possibility in the cathedral, but no, surely not—that would be too much of a coincidence—but it would be somebody *like* Violet Sephotho, no doubt. Gaborone was full of aspiring Violet Sephothos.

Mma Mateleke shook her head. "No. I have not heard her name."

"What do you know about her? Do you know where she lives?"

Mma Mateleke shrugged. "I have not seen her. In fact, Mma, I have no actual proof. All I'm saying to you is that I *think* that he's having an affair. You're the one who can find the proof for me."

The waitress arrived and placed a tray down on the table. She was a young woman, barely into her twenties, and she seemed keen to please. Mma Mateleke seemed indifferent to her, but Mma Ramotswe thanked her, and told her that the tea smelled very good. The waitress smiled wordlessly and went back inside.

Mma Ramotswe warned her friend about jumping to conclusions. "It's a very common fear for us women," she said. "Most women worry that their husband's eye might start to wander. And his hands too, Mma. That's natural enough. But you shouldn't imagine that he's having an affair unless you have some reason to think that. Have you got any reasons?"

"Reasons? You're asking me for reasons? I'm telling you, Mma, any woman whose husband is carrying on just *knows* what's going on. You feel it. He sits there smiling and you think, *What has he got to smile about?* And then you suddenly find out that he has bought himself some of that aftershave stuff and is putting it on his face. You think, *So why is he putting that stuff on now when he never used to put it on? Never?* That is the sort of thing you think, Mma, and it all adds up. Then you say to yourself, *He is having an affair—I know it.*"

Mma Ramotswe felt unhappy about the lack of proof, but that was as a detective. As a woman she knew exactly what Mma Mateleke was talking about, and she knew, too, that her fears were likely to be well founded. Men had affairs; that is what men did, and even if she had previously assumed that Herbert Mateleke was a settled, rather conservative man, she had to admit that even settled, conservative men had affairs. In fact, they were often the worst of all.

There was another thing that was worrying her. Herbert Mateleke might not be a close friend, but he was the husband of a friend, and that was worrying. Clovis Andersen had advice to give on this topic and, as usual, it was wise counsel. *Do not act for friends if you can possibly avoid it,* he wrote in *The Principles of Private Detection.* And then he continued, *And the reason for this? Experience has taught me that if you act for a friend you will take the friend's perspective on things. You will see things that the friend wants you to see because you are emotionally involved in the case. So here is Rule 32: Remember when to say no to a case. Better to lose a fee than to lose a friend.*

Mma Ramotswe sipped at her tea. Mma Mateleke had yet to

ask her to investigate on her behalf, but she was sure that such a request was coming. And it was.

"I know that you are very busy, Mma Ramotswe," said Mma Mateleke, adding, "Everybody is busy these days. The whole of Botswana is busy."

Mma Ramotswe considered this last observation. Was the whole of Botswana busy? Certainly people seemed busy enough in Gaborone, but she was not so sure about the country areas. In fact, there were many people out in the country who did not appear very busy at all. These were the people who sat outside their houses and watched the cattle amble past, or those who stood under trees and spoke with friends, or who put a chair somewhere in the sun and then sat on it. And that, surely, was how life should be. What was the point of rushing around as if everything had to be done today when there was plenty of time ahead of you, years and years, if you were lucky?

"But even if you are busy," Mma Mateleke continued, "you might still find the time to do this favour I'm asking of you, my sister."

My sister—the two words were very powerful, and Mma Ramotswe knew it. This was an appeal to something that went beyond the normal incidence of friendship. This was an appeal to the African sense of mutual help, and the duty to give such help. You did not call somebody your sister unless you believed in all that—as Mma Ramotswe did. And Mma Mateleke, of course, knew that Mma Ramotswe believed.

"You can ask me," said Mma Ramotswe, "and I shall say yes." The words came out almost without having been thought about, but she knew that she was bound by them.

Mma Mateleke, who had been sitting with shoulders hunched in tension, now relaxed. "Please will you find this evidence that I need. Please will you find who is this woman he is having an affair with. Her name. Where she lives. What she looks like. It will not be hard for you."

Mma Ramotswe had to acknowledge that it would not. It was difficult to conceal an affair in Gaborone, as there were not all that many places to go, and where there were a thousand eyes and ears. If Herbert Mateleke was seeing somebody else, then she would find out quite quickly. There was something, though, that was still troubling her, and she now raised this with her friend. "May I ask you, Mma, what you intend to do with the information, once you have it? I always ask clients that—it is not just you."

This inquiry seemed to take Mma Mateleke by surprise; it was as if the answer were so obvious that the question need not have been asked. "It is so that I can divorce him," she said abruptly. "Why else would I want to know?"

Several other reasons crossed Mma Ramotswe's mind, but she did not reveal them. So that you might forgive him, she thought. So that you might plead with the other woman not to break up your marriage, and might succeed. So that you might reflect on why he feels it necessary to have an extramarital affair in the first place.

"Very well," said Mma Ramotswe. "I will look into this. I don't think that it will take long. And . . ." She hesitated.

"And what, Mma?"

"And it may be that Herbert is innocent," she said. "After all, some men are, you know."

CHAPTER TEN

SOME PEOPLE JUST SIT IN
THEIR CARS

MMA RAMOTSWE was in a thoughtful mood when she returned to the office. Mr. J.L.B. Matekoni—and Mma Potokwane too, for that matter—had occasionally said that she had a soft heart and that "no" was not one of the words that her heart understood. She had laughed at the appraisal; in her view, Mr. J.L.B. Matekoni was every bit as soft-hearted as she was—he would never turn anybody away, and would fix even the most mechanically hopeless cars—and as for Mma Potokwane, well, everybody knew that she would do anything for those orphans she looked after, and if that was not a sign of a soft heart, then what was? So although she knew that she should have declined to help Mma Mateleke, she also knew that she could not refuse her friend. But she did not relish the task that lay ahead of her, as it would involve watching somebody she knew, and that was not a good idea.

It was easy enough watching a stranger. One could sit in one's van and pretend to be reading, or even sleeping. Plenty of people did that: they sat in their cars, talking to friends or listening to the car radio, or even just sitting. Nobody would have reason to be suspicious of that. But if one sat in one's van out-side the house of somebody one knew, and then followed him as he turned out of the drive, one would obviously be noticed. She imagined the scene, as Herbert Mateleke asked her, "Mma Ramotswe, I saw you sitting outside my house yesterday after-noon. It was you, wasn't it? I'm sure it was. And then when I drove off down the road, you followed me. Perhaps you wanted me to show you the way, Mma . . ." And she would not know what to say, but would mumble something about how small the town was, in spite of being so big, and how easy it was to bump into people one knew along the road, just as easy, in fact, as in one of those tiny villages . . .

By the time she had reached the shared premises of the No. 1 Ladies' Detective Agency and Tlokweng Road Speedy Motors, she had decided that she could not possibly follow Herbert Mateleke, and that the only thing to do was to stick to the procedure that she used in so many of her cases. If she wanted to find out the answer to anything, then she simply had to ask somebody. It was that simple, it really was, and she had done this on numerous occasions, with conspicuously success-ful results. Sometimes the answer she received was direct; on other occasions it was not so direct, but was nonetheless unam-biguous. She remembered how, in one investigation into pilfer-ing in an office—disappearing petty cash and so on—she had simply called the staff to attend a meeting. Then, as they all stood before her, some twelve people, she had said, "Now then, everybody, the manager says that money has been stolen, and I wonder who's doing it?" And immediately all pairs of eyes had turned and looked at one member of staff, who had stared steadfastly at the ground. People know, she thought; they know things that they might be unwilling to say. Nobody in that office would have been willing to denounce the offender openly, but we reveal so much through our eyes. Our eyes, she thought, show what is in the heart.

That experience, called to mind as she made her way into the office, pointed the way. Yes, she would go and speak to Herbert Mateleke and talk to him about somebody else having an affair, and his eyes would give her all the information she needed. After that, she might be in a position to ask him, rather more directly, whether she could help him in any way with any difficulties he was experiencing. But then there would be an additional problem: he might speak to her in confidence, and that would mean that she could not reveal what he said to Mma Mateleke, and she was now, in a way, her client, and . . . and all that underlined the fact that she should not have said yes in the first place. She sighed; Clovis Andersen was useful, but he usually only came up with general propositions. There was nowhere in the book where you could go and get concrete advice about a situation such as this. Oh, to be able to speak to somebody like Clovis Andersen in person—but he was somewhere far away, and he would never have heard of Mma Ramotswe and the No. 1 Ladies' Detective Agency, nor of Botswana, perhaps, and he might even be late by now. The back cover of *The Principles of Private Detection,* so well thumbed in the hands of Mma Ramotswe and Mma Makutsi, said nothing about who the author was, other than to describe him as a "man of vast experience in the field," and to show a photograph of a man with greying hair and a pair of horn-rimmed spectacles. That was all; there was no mention of an office, or a place, or a family; and the photograph had no background to give any clue as to where he was—which was deliberate, perhaps. The great Clovis Andersen would not want people like her, she thought, pestering him with questions about how to deal with the husband of a friend who might be having an affair, or who might simply be trying to escape a nagging wife, as some husbands were known to do.

Mma Makutsi, now back from compassionate leave, would not have guessed that her employer had been entertaining these doubts. Mma Ramotswe did not believe in burdening others with her worries, and so she greeted her assistant with a cheery smile and a suggestion that she might think of putting on the kettle for late-morning tea. She had just had tea, of course, but that had been a business cup of tea, and that did not count.

Mma Makutsi looked up from her desk, and Mma Ramotswe knew immediately that something was wrong. Phuti, she thought. He was still in hospital. He had taken a turn for the worse. Infection had set in. He had fallen. Perhaps he had got out of bed and forgotten that he had only one foot now, and . . .

"He is out of hospital," said Mma Makutsi.

Mma Ramotswe clapped her hands. "Oh, Mma, that is very good news. Very good news indeed." She paused; Mma Makutsi's expression still did not seem like that of one whose fiancé has just been discharged from hospital.

"He is at his aunt's place," said Mma Makutsi glumly. "You know that woman. She has taken him."

Mma Ramotswe sat down at her desk. "That must be because they often do not want to let people go out by themselves," she said. "They like to hand them over to the care of relatives, so that they will be looked after." She watched the effect of her words on Mma Makutsi. The younger woman remained glum.

"Is a fiancée not a relative, Mma?" Mma Makutsi asked indignantly. "Does a ring mean nothing these days? Is the lady who is going to look after him for the rest of his life not close enough to be able to take care of him when he comes out of hospital with only one . . ." Her voice faltered, and Mma Ramotswe began to rise from her desk. The remaining words were drowned in tears. "With only one foot," Mma Makutsi wailed. "And the other foot just . . . just thrown away like some old rubbish . . . And he will have to have crutches to begin with, and I would help him . . . And he is a good man, Mma, and it's so unfair that an accident happens to a good man when there are all these bad men walking about the place with two complete legs and not having accidents . . ."

It was a river, a torrent, of grief; grief for what had happened to Phuti Radiphuti, but for other things too, things that were under the surface, but which rose up now to express their pain too, old things that went back a long time. Mma Ramotswe sensed this, and moved quickly to Mma Makutsi's side, putting her arms about her, trying to comfort her. There were tears on Mma Makutsi's face, and these were streaming down her cheeks, taking with them the cream that she put on her skin, for the problems she had with that.

"Oh, Mma, you are crying. He is out of hospital—that is the important thing. She must have gone and told them that she was the aunt. Phuti would not have had much say in it."

"They should not have let that woman take him away," sobbed Mma Makutsi. "She has taken him to her place and she will poison him."

Mma Ramotswe could not stop herself from gasping. "Poison him? Mma, what are you saying?"

"She will poison him," Mma Makutsi repeated. But her voice lacked conviction; she knew how outrageous her accusation was.

"You must not say things like that," Mma Ramotswe chided her. "You are upset, Mma, I can tell that, but it is very dangerous to talk about poisoning people. It is very dangerous, Mma. Do you hear me?" It was a serious point; Mma Makutsi may have been upset, but in a country where, for all its good points, there lingered in the minds of some a belief in witchcraft and poisoning, it was explosive talk. And Mma Makutsi realised this, and reminded herself that she was not some superstitious and uneducated person from the back of beyond, but an assistant detective in the modern city of Gaborone and a graduate, moreover, of the Botswana Secretarial College (with ninety-seven per cent).

"Maybe she won't poison him," Mma Makutsi sniffed. "But why did she say, when I telephoned her, that I could not speak to him? She said he is resting, and that she would see if he could phone me later."

Mma Ramotswe crossed the room to the shelf where the kettle was kept. Tea was often the solution in fraught moments, and she was sure that Mma Makutsi would think more reasonably once tea had been served.

"Perhaps she is merely telling the truth. After you have come out of hospital it is always a good idea to rest. You do not go and play football the moment you come out of hospital . . ." She tailed off. The words had come out without her thinking much about them; football was a very unfortunate choice, in the circumstances. She corrected herself. "I mean, you do not run around . . ." It was another tactless choice of words.

Mma Ramotswe glanced over her shoulder as she put tea into the pot. Mma Makutsi was staring at her.

"What is this about football, Mma Ramotswe? Phuti has never played football. And how can you run around when you have only one foot, Mma?"

"This is good tea," said Mma Ramotswe, in an attempt to divert attention from football, and feet, and running. "You will enjoy it, I think. Five Roses tea. It is very good."

"I have always used that tea," said Mma Makutsi stiffly. "I do not think this will be any different. But why talk about running around, Mma? He will not be running."

"It was just a way of saying that after you come out of hospital you have to take things easily. Mr. J.L.B. Matekoni knows a man who went into hospital and then came out and immediately went on a charity walk for the Lions Club, and now he is late."

"He became late on the walk?"

Mma Ramotswe nodded. "They said to him that he should not go, that he was still weak, but he would not listen. He was struck by lightning."

"And that is how he became late?"

"Yes." It happened, and surprisingly often. The powerful electrical storms that built up in the rainy season discharged great bolts of lightning that ended the lives of unfortunates out in the open; in a landscape of low trees and wide spaces, a man might be the most tempting conductor.

Mma Makutsi frowned. "But I do not see what that has got to do with coming out of hospital. There are always people being struck by lightning. There was a man in Bobonong last year. He was getting his chickens in out of the rain and then he was late. Only his shoes were left."

It was not a cheerful conversation, but it had at least distracted Mma Makutsi from the subject of Phuti. And over tea, they talked about other matters and other people, including Mrs. Grant.

"I have made a decision," announced Mma Ramotswe. "We are going to Maun."

Mma Makutsi was enthusiastic. "This will be a business trip?" she asked.

"It will, Mma," said Mma Ramotswe. "We shall go up in my

van and stay with cousins of Mr. J.L.B. Matekoni. They live just
outside Maun. Then we can carry out our investigations."

Mma Makutsi beamed with pleasure. Dabbing at her make-
up with a small lace handkerchief, she sought to repair the dam-
age that the tears had caused. "I have never been on a business
trip," she said. "This is very good news."

It was the reaction that Mma Ramotswe had hoped for. It
would do her assistant a great deal of good, she thought, to have
her mind taken off Phuti's woes. And during that time the aunt—
difficult though she may be—could look after her nephew. That
would help too, Mma Ramotswe felt; people were awkward for a
reason, as often as not, and the reason for awkwardness here was
probably that the aunt felt her role was threatened by Mma
Makutsi. If she believed herself to be needed on this occasion,
perhaps she might feel less insecure. Perhaps . . .

"Of course, all expenses will be paid," Mma Ramotswe
went on.

This clearly pleased Mma Makutsi. "Yes," she said approv-
ingly. "That is the general rule with business trips. They told us
about that at the Botswana Secretarial College." She did not
mention that they had also warned: Do not go on business trips
with your boss. Of course they had in mind a situation where a
male employer invited a female secretary to accompany him on a
business trip. That was an invitation to disaster in most cases, as
more might be expected of the secretary than mere dictation.
This was quite different, of course; a business trip with a female
boss was just a business trip. But she wondered what expenses
there would be. If they were travelling up to Maun in Mma
Ramotswe's van, then there would be no tickets to be bought, and
Mma Ramotswe had never asked her to pay for any petrol. There
would be no hotel, if they were staying with Mr. J.L.B. Mate-

koni's cousins, and she would not need any new clothes or . . . Shoes?

"That is very nice," Mma Makutsi said brightly. "You mean incidental expenses?"

Mma Ramotswe nodded, cautiously.

"Such as shoe expenses?" Mma Makutsi ventured.

There was a silence. "I'm not sure what shoe expenses are, Mma," said Mma Ramotswe. "If your shoes are damaged up there, then of course the office will pay for them to be fixed. But that is very unlikely, I think. I was thinking more of . . ." She was about to list the purchase of the occasional snack on the journey, and the cost of food up in Maun, but she did not have the chance to complete what she was saying.

"It is very wild up there," said Mma Makutsi firmly. "It is the Delta, as you know. It is not Gaborone, where there are streets and where the paths are safe. This is the bush, Mma, and you cannot wear town shoes in bush like that. You will fall into an anteater hole, or something like that. There are many things like that in the Okavango Delta." And then, with a final flourish, a petard of Mma Ramotswe's own making now hoist, "That is well known, Mma."

Mma Ramotswe struggled to contain herself. "What do you have in mind, Mma Makutsi?" And then, with what she felt was a very timely move, she said, "I shall be very happy to lend you a pair of my stout shoes, Mma. You cannot wear those nice green shoes of yours up in the Delta," and added, "even if they would be very good camouflage." Irresistibly, irreverently, she imagined Mma Makutsi moving through the thick grass, her feet now successfully camouflaged and invisible, but her large glasses catching the sun and giving everything away.

Mma Makutsi shook her head. "That is very kind of you, Mma, and I am very grateful. I would not want you to think that I did not appreciate your offer." She paused to take breath. "Your shoes have always struck me as being very sensible, and will be very good up in the Delta. There is no doubt about that. But there is a problem here. Your feet are very good feet, Mma, but they are not small feet. My own feet are not the smallest feet in Gaborone, but they are not quite as large as your own feet are. And that means I cannot wear your shoes, as they would fall off every time I took a step."

Mma Ramotswe bit her lip. Phuti Radiphuti was well off, he could afford to buy his fiancée new shoes, and she did not think it appropriate that shoes should be treated as a business expense.

"I was thinking of a pair of those boots that they have for ladies," Mma Makutsi suggested. "You've seen them, Mma. You know those ones which go up to the ankles—or just above, and have laces at the front. They're usually made of light brown suede. They're very smart, but also very practical. Those are the shoes that I'll need." Then she added, "And I know where to buy them, Mma. I have seen a pair for three hundred pula. That is a very good buy."

Mma Ramotswe looked out of the window. She knew of Mma Makutsi's interest in shoes. It was not all that long ago that she had acquired yet another pair, only six months or so after she had bought the previous pair. With this new green pair, how many pairs of shoes did her assistant now have? There were the blue shoes, the red shoes, the shoes that looked as if they had been made out of crocodile skin, or something similar (Mma Makutsi had not been amused by Mma Ramotswe's suggestion that it might be anteater or even porcupine skin), although not much had been seen of those after they proved so fashionable as to be impossible to walk in. On the whole, she did not need yet another pair of shoes, and yet what she said was true: one could not walk about the bush in town shoes. But it was also true that the only reason Mma Makutsi needed to walk about the bush was because Mma Ramotswe had invited her to go with her to Maun.

She turned round. "All right, Mma. You can take the money from the petty cash. Go and get those shoes."

She felt better immediately for saying this. Mma Makutsi was a hard worker. She had not had much in this life, and she had worked diligently for everything she did have, including her shoes. This was a very distressing time, and if she could be helped through it by indulging her passion for shoes, then that was, perhaps, something that Mma Ramotswe owed her.

Mma Makutsi's gratitude was plain to see. "Oh, Mma, that is very good news. Why don't you come with me right now, and we can go and get those boots? And some boots for you too."

Mma Ramotswe raised her hands in protest. "I do not need boots, Mma. I've got my comfortable flat shoes. You could walk across the Kalahari—and back—in those shoes of mine."

"And what if you stand on a snake, Mma, while you're walking across the Kalahari? What then?"

"I will be very careful," said Mma Ramotswe. "I've been walking about Botswana for a long time and I have not yet stood on a snake. And we're not going to the Kalahari. We're going to the Okavango Delta."

"Careful, Mma!" Mma Makutsi warned. "There is always a first time for everything. There is something called the law of averages—you may have heard of it. It says that if you haven't trodden on a snake yet, then you may tread on one soon-soon."

THEY DROVE IN THE VAN to Riverwalk. There was a small parking incident, in which Mma Ramotswe narrowly avoided scraping the wing of the next-door car, a gleaming piece of German machinery. It was a narrow escape, and Mma Makutsi could not avoid a sharp intake of breath as the two vehicles had their close encounter.

"That car is far too big," said Mma Ramotswe. "It is taking up too much room. Soon there will be not enough room in Botswana for the rest of us if these big cars keep coming."

"Maybe we should have given it a bit more room, Mma," her assistant said. "I'm not criticising your driving, but it is sometimes a good idea to give big cars a bit more room."

Mma Ramotswe was having none of that. "You are not a big person just because you have a big car. All people are entitled to the same amount of room."

That settled, they made their way into the covered walkway between the shops. Halfway along, beside a shop selling clothing, was a shop devoted to tents, mosquito nets, sheath knives, and the other requirements of those setting off into the bush. Mma Ramotswe's eye was drawn to a stand displaying compasses, and a booklet entitled *How Not to Get Lost in the Bush*. She picked up the booklet and paged through it. There was a section on how to find north, south, east, and west. She smiled as she read this; it could not have been intended for any local readers. Everybody she knew was fully aware of exactly which way north lay— because that was the direction in which the Francistown Road ran; South Africa was over there, beyond Tlokweng, to the east; Lobatse lay in the south; and to the west was the Kalahari, which anybody with a nose could *smell*, apart from anything else, because when the wind came from that quarter it was a fragrant mixture of dryness and emptiness and waving grass. But she had to acknowledge that if one did not know these things—and a visitor could hardly be expected to—then this book, with its diagrams and its explanation of how to track the passage of the sun by inserting a stick into the ground, was well worth its eighty-pula cover price.

The assistant approached them, and Mma Makutsi pointed to the boots, which were prominently displayed on a shelf behind the counter. Each woman gave her size, and the appropriate boxes were fetched from a cupboard.

"They will be very comfortable," said Mma Makutsi. "You will not regret this, Mma."

Mma Ramotswe was not so sure. She had the distinct feeling that she was being pushed into the purchase of these boots by Mma Makutsi, and she did not think that she could legitimately pass the cost on to the client. She could hardly add to the bill *Boots: 600 pula.* Any client receiving that would be perfectly within his rights to challenge it, and if it could not be passed on, then she would have to pay it herself.

The assistant returned with boxes tucked under her arm. As the boots were unpacked, Mma Ramotswe noticed something about Mma Makutsi's expression—a look of anticipation that went far beyond anything one might normally expect. It was the look that one might see on the face of a child about to be given a treat, a look that spoke of sheer, uncomplicated pleasure and excitement. We lose that look, she thought, as we get older; we forget what it is like to be so thrilled. This, then, was the look of a woman who *loved* shoes.

Mma Makutsi was attended to first. The boots were perfect, she said, and she would take them, or rather Mma Ramotswe would.

The assistant turned to Mma Ramotswe. "Your feet are much bigger," she said. "These boots might be too small. But let us try, Mma."

It was a slightly tight fit, but the assistant pointed out that suede gave under pressure and that they would fit perfectly well after a day or two's use.

"Then we shall take those as well," said Mma Makutsi. "That is: one pair for me and one pair for this lady. Two pairs."

Mma Ramotswe threw her a glance. There were times, she thought, when Mma Makutsi forgot that she was an assistant detective, not a director of the agency; ninety-seven per cent notwithstanding, she was her assistant, and assistants did not make the decisions on important purchases. She was not one to put anybody down, and certainly not when Mma Makutsi turned to her to say, "Mma Ramotswe, you have been very kind. There are very few people who are lucky enough to have a boss as generous as you are. This is not just me saying this, Mma; I am speaking from my heart, from here." And she pointed to her chest, and Mma Ramotswe smiled and thanked her, and told her that she was glad that they were both now well prepared for their trip. "I am very happy, Mma," she said, which she was, and she was pleased with her new boots too, which she thought made her look quite a bit younger, and made her feel more agile.

She paid the bill, counting out twelve fifty-pula notes that had more or less depleted the office's petty cash. Then, as they were about to leave the shop, Mma Makutsi took Mma Ramotswe's arm. "There is a man staring at you," she said. "Look, out there. Near that bench. He has a familiar face. Who is he, Mma?"

Mma Ramotswe looked through the shop window to the walkway outside. Mr. Herbert Mateleke, part-time reverend, suspected adulterer, was standing in the shade, staring at her. It was almost as if he was following her, as she had earlier on imagined herself following him.

_____

CHAPTER ELEVEN

COFFEE WITH A PART-TIME REVEREND

So, RRA," Mma Ramotswe said as she came out of the shop. "So, here you are standing, thinking about what to say to the faithful."

Mma Makutsi now remembered where she had seen this man: he had been on television, talking about a plan to raise one million pula for some ambitious project—a flying-doctor plane, or something of that sort. There were so many people with projects, she thought, and most of them sounded very worthy. But how did one decide where one's charity would go? It was very difficult. And then the further thought came that she did not give very much—in fact, she gave nothing, even though now she could spare one or two pula, her single-girl's mite, so to speak. She would start giving one day, after she had received a little bit more herself; then she would give.

Herbert Mateleke laughed. It was a short laugh, though—that of one who had been distracted from something grave, and needed to get back to more serious thoughts. "I was not thinking of higher things, Mma. I was trying to make out whether it was you I saw in the shop. With the light like this, you see, the glass reflects and you cannot see exactly who is on the other side. Now I see it is you."

"And my secretary, Mma Makutsi. We have been . . ."

"Assistant detective," interjected Mma Makutsi, giving Mma Ramotswe a disapproving glance. "We have been buying equipment for a case."

Herbert Mateleke nodded distractedly. "Yes, of course. You must need a lot of equipment." He paused, gathering his thoughts for an aphorism. "We need a lot of equipment to find out the truth in this world."

Mma Ramotswe raised an eyebrow. "Do you think so, Rra? I think that all we need in order to know the truth is these." She pointed to her eyes. And then, pointing to her nose, "And this. This is a very big help in finding out what is true and what is not. Don't you agree, Rra?"

There was no edge to what she said, but as she spoke to Herbert Mateleke she could not forget the fact that, at least in his wife's eyes, he stood accused of having an affair. And that shirt—that bright blue shirt—was that the sort of shirt one expected a successful businessman and part-time reverend to wear? Or was it the shirt of a man who was trying to make himself a little bit more colourful, rather more interesting to women? She knew the warning signs with middle-aged men—they were like a set of traffic lights that glowed brightly in the dark. Greater attention to personal grooming? Bad sign. Pulling-in of the stomach to conceal paunch? Bad sign. Purchase of a more powerful car in bright red? Very, very bad sign.

Of course, the shirt could be interpreted in various ways. It was a loose-fitting, open-neck shirt of the sort worn by Nelson Mandela. Such shirts were not tucked into one's trousers, but hung about the waist, allowing for air to circulate. They suited older men very well, those on whose physique prosperity, and particularly a diet of good Botswana beef, might have taken its toll, and they were perfect, of course, for Mr. Mandela himself, who lent them that grace and dignity that came so naturally to him. You might conclude, thought Mma Ramotswe, that Mr. Mateleke was wearing this shirt because it was comfortable and paid tribute, perhaps, to that most gracious of men who had popularised the style. Or you might conclude that here was a man who was paying attention to his clothes because he was having an affair. You might reach for either of these conclusions, but if you were a detective, and you had been approached by the wife of the man in question, who had given voice to her own suspicions, then you would be excused, surely, for reaching the second, less charitable of these conclusions.

Herbert Mateleke now leaned forward, as if to impart a confidence to Mma Ramotswe. She thought quickly: if he wanted to talk, then she should encourage him. This was exactly the sort of development that could make a potentially awkward enquiry that much easier.

"Mma Makutsi," said Mma Ramotswe. "I think that you should take the rest of the day off. Why don't you go and do some shopping?"

Mma Makutsi could see what the situation was, and reacted accordingly, and with consummate professionalism. "It was just what I was hoping to do, Mma. Thank you very much." She nodded to Herbert Mateleke. "It was very good to meet you, Rra, and I do like your shirt. It suits you very well."

Herbert Mateleke acknowledged the compliment, but his acknowledgement was perfunctory, a matter of form; it was clear that there was something on his mind. As Mma Makutsi went off, Mma Ramotswe looked at her watch. "I am a bit hungry for some reason, Rra. I do not know why."

He seized the opportunity. "But I am hungry too, Mma, and there is that place round the corner, near the bottle store."

"I am told their food is very good," said Mma Ramotswe.

"I would like to take you to lunch, Mma Ramotswe, if you will let me."

The offer was accepted, and the two walked the short distance to the café. Nothing was said on this walk—or nothing significant—and it was not until they had sat down at their table and were examining the menu that Herbert Mateleke unburdened himself.

"You know something, Mma Ramotswe?" he began. "I am not a happy man."

"But . . ."

He held up a hand. "Let me explain, Mma. I am a person who is always telling other people that they must rejoice and love the Lord. Alleluia, alleluia! That is what I am always saying. And when I see people who are happy, I say, 'Alleluia! You are living in goodness and light!' But all the time, Mma, inside me there is just an unhappiness and . . ."—he paused, staring straight into Mma Ramotswe's eyes—". . . and doubt."

For a moment she said nothing. She knew that reverends sometimes had doubts about what they professed to believe, and that this could not be easy for them. It would be like telling somebody all the time to do something that one would not do oneself. But was she the person to address his doubts? Surely he should go and speak to somebody who knew something about these matters—another reverend, perhaps, or a teacher of theology. Of course, there were all sorts of other doubts . . . doubts about marriage? Was saying that one had doubts a way of saying that one was thinking of leaving one's spouse? Mma Ramotswe was not sure; these days there were so many ways of describing unpleasant things and making them sound quite pleasant. Nobody ran away from their responsibilities any more—they were said to have gone off to find themselves. Nobody dismissed anybody from their job any more—they let them go. What if they said, "But I do not want to go!" The only reply would be, "But I'm still going to let you!" It showed what nonsense these silly expressions were—at least Setswana did not have them: words in Setswana meant exactly what they said.

"I am worried about my wife," Herbert Mateleke blurted out. "I have started to doubt her."

Mma Ramotswe looked down at the tablecloth. He was doubting her? But he was the one who was meant to be having the affair! Or was this a part of the modern business of turning everything on its head, of making bad sound good and good sound bad, or at least very dull?

At last she asked, "Why is this, Rra? Why are you doubting her?"

Her question was clear enough, but he appeared to need some time to answer it. When the answer came, however, it was unambiguous. "I think that she is seeing another man."

Mma Ramotswe could not conceal her surprise. This was not the way she had thought the encounter would go. She should be trying to find out whether he was having an affair, and now here was he about to ask her—and she was sure the request would not be long in coming—to find out whether Mma Mateleke was seeing somebody.

He was staring at her. "You look surprised, Mma. I suppose I can understand."

She gathered her thoughts. "Yes, I am a bit surprised, Rra. I cannot deny that."

He sighed. "That's the trouble, isn't it? If I went to anybody and said, 'Do you realise that my wife is having an affair?' they would be very surprised. They would say, 'But she is a very respectable lady, Rra. She is that well-known midwife. And you are a part-time reverend.'And so on. That is what they would say."

Mma Ramotswe asked him why he thought Mma Mateleke was seeing somebody. Did he have any proof? She was trying to remember what Mr. J.L.B. Matekoni had told her. Something about a car and the Lobatse Road. The Lobatse Road was not a good place to conduct an affair; it was far too busy. Now some small, out-of-the-way road, some road that wandered away to a distant cattle post, or off into the Kalahari until it disappeared in the sand, that road would be the place for a lovers' meeting.

He shook his head. "I have no proof. I have no letters filled with kisses and things like that. But I have seen her talking to a man. I saw her outside the Botswana Book Centre one day. She was talking to a man."

Mma Ramotswe smiled. "But that is nothing, Rra! Many women talk to men. They may know a man from work, or something like that. Yes, maybe she knew him from work."

Herbert Mateleke shook his head. "She is a midwife, Mma, as you know. Men do not have babies. Yet." He hesitated. "Although there are many men these days who want to have babies, I think."

Mma Ramotswe smiled at that. There were so many different sorts of men these days, that was true, and she wondered whether she might have to change her views of men, which were based, she had to admit, on the idea of traditional men; there were plenty of men today who seemed to be interested in things like clothing and hairstyles, even here in Botswana. And there was a whole generation, she had to acknowledge—reluctantly—who knew very little about cattle, and, shockingly, *were not interested in learning*. If there was one thing that would upset her father, the late Obed Ramotswe, were he by some miracle to come back and see Botswana today, it would be that. He could take the rudeness of the day—not that Botswana was nearly as bad as many places—and he could take the materialism of the day, but she did not think that he would understand this lack of interest in the land and in the cattle. "But this is Botswana!" he would say to these young people. "You are Batswana and you have no interest in cattle? How can that be!"

This was not the time, though, to reflect on change in the world. This was the time to try to allay Herbert Mateleke's highly unlikely suspicions about his wife. Those suspicions, of course, spoke volumes on the issue of whether he himself was having an affair. He was not. A husband who was having an affair would not have the time or the interest in his wife to work himself into a state over her fidelity or otherwise. No, the most likely explanation here was that these two people, perhaps having become a bit stale in their marriage, were imagining things—on both sides.

"Even if she does not work with men," Mma Ramotswe pointed out, "there could be many other reasons for her to talk to a man. What about the daddies—the men who have fathered the children she has delivered? Do you not think they would have good memories of her, and want to tell her how the children are doing?"

She waited for him to answer, but he merely looked glumly over the top of her head. So she continued, "I do not think for one moment—not for one moment—that you can draw such a serious conclusion just from seeing her talking to a man. In public. In the open. For heaven's sake, Rra, what if Mr. J.L.B. Matekoni were to see you and me sitting here having food together? Would he say to himself, that man, that Herbert Mateleke, is having an affair with my wife? Of course he would not. He would say: that is Mma Ramotswe having a snack with her friend's husband. Then he would ask himself: I wonder what they are eating. Is it good? That is what he would think, Rra. And that is what *you* should think too."

Herbert Mateleke stopped staring over the top of her head, lowering his eyes to meet hers. "But there are other things. There are other things that make me think this."

"Such as? Are you sure you are not letting your imagination run away with itself?"

"I am not. We used to go for walks together. I used to go with her to the supermarket. Now she says that she is too busy. She says that I should get on with my preaching and let her get on with the things she has to do."

Wives lost interest in their husbands, Mma Ramotswe reflected. Sometimes husbands did not notice this, but it could be rather difficult if the husband was the clinging, dependent type of man. She studied Herbert Mateleke for a moment, asking herself what it would be like to be married to him. It was something she did from time to time, and for the most part she reached the conclusion that it would actually be rather hard being married to most men; not that she was fussy, of course. And she expected that most men would probably not wish to be married to her—that was only fair if she did not want to be married to them. Mr. J.L.B. Matekoni was perfect, as far as she was concerned—he was so understanding and considerate, compared with most men.

She would definitely not like to be married to Herbert Mateleke. It was not that he was a boorish or unpleasant man—far from it. The problem was that he was a reverend, and she imagined that he would always be preaching at his wife, telling her what to do. And if that were the case, then it would be no great surprise, perhaps, if Mma Mateleke were to feel a little bit trapped, and to try to do at least some things on her own.

How might one put that tactfully? Mma Ramotswe took a

deep breath. "Women need some room for themselves, Rra," she ventured. "You know how it is."

He looked at her blankly. "Some room, Mma? She has a great deal of space. Our house is very big. My wife is never crowded."

"I don't mean room in that sense," said Mma Ramotswe. "I mean room to do things by herself. We all want to do that, Rra. It's natural."

He stared at her without expression. He has not understood, she thought.

"You don't like being with other people all the time, do you, Rra? Don't you sometimes feel like getting away from everybody and taking a walk by yourself? Surely you feel that?"

"But she is my wife," said Herbert Mateleke. "Why should she not want to be with me all the time?"

He had neither listened nor understood, thought Mma Ramotswe. Of course Mma Mateleke would want to get away from her husband. She simply wanted to breathe, as all women do. And men too. We all needed to breathe. She would like to point this out to Herbert Mateleke, but she was not sure that he would understand. The realisation came to her that this man, for all his success and his following, was actually not very bright. Mma Mateleke was an intelligent woman, and perhaps she had simply grown bored with this rather slow, literal man. But that did not mean she would go out and have an affair; that was surely unlikely. Apart from anything else, Mma Mateleke was simply *too busy* delivering babies to have an affair.

"Let me tell you what I think, Rra," she said. She was suddenly businesslike. He was looking for advice; well, she would give it, first to him, and then later to Mma Mateleke. She would bang their heads together and say, "Listen, you are both worrying about something that is not happening. But sort this out before you drift apart and the thing that you worry about really does happen. Listen to one another. Find out how each of you is feeling. And above all, stop worrying."

Of course, she knew that it was almost always pointless telling somebody to stop worrying. We all did it; we told friends not to worry because their worries seemed small, unimportant things to us, and we knew that such problems were never solved by brooding over them. But people never stopped worrying simply because they were told to. They listened, perhaps, and told you that they would stop, but they carried on nonetheless. That was true, Mma Ramotswe thought, of most advice we gave; people often listened, but only very rarely acted on what was said to them. "Thank you, Mma," they said. "That is very wise." And then they went on to do exactly what they had planned to do in the first place. People were very strange. Mma Ramotswe had decided that early in her career, and had seen nothing to disabuse her of that notion. People were very strange.

But this was not a time to question the whole idea of giving advice; this was a time to give it. "This is what I think, Rra," she said. "I do not think that your wife is having an affair. I think that you are worrying for no reason. And I also think that she might be worrying about you! Yes! So the two of you should sit down and talk together. Then go out to the President Hotel and have dinner together. Pretend that you're twenty-five again and out on a date. That is what you must do."

He listened to her carefully, and this time he appeared to be taking in what she was saying. Sometimes reverends did not listen to others, she had observed, because they thought that there was nobody else who could tell them anything. But Mma Ramotswe's plain talking had had an effect; he was listening, and he was taking it in. Good, she thought. This is a very good result.

No affairs. No unhappiness. Nothing. And no fee, of course, as Mma Mateleke had not actually consulted her as a detective, but had prevailed upon her as a friend. No fee.

WHILE MMA RAMOTSWE was sitting in the café with Herbert Mateleke, Mma Makutsi set off out of the office for the rest of the afternoon—and why not, given that all her filing was completely up to date and all the bills, such as they were, had been sent out? What was the point of her sitting in the office waiting for five o'clock, when she could go home and wait until five o'clock, when she would go to see Phuti at his aunt's house? To pass the time she would make a cup of tea and read a copy of the magazine she had bought at Exclusive Books. This magazine was full of delights, and she could hardly wait to start turning its glossy, newly printed pages. The cover promised an article on the doings of some big stars; that always made for interesting reading, as the big stars were often up to no good. She liked to look at the pictures that accompanied such articles, and to study the clothes that these big stars wore. They dressed expensively, these people, and as for their shoes . . .

She looked down at her feet. She had decided to wear the boots she had just bought so that they would be worn in by the time she went up to the Delta. Now, making her way along Odi Drive, she felt very pleased with the comfort of her new footwear. She had read that ankle support was very important, and she had thought at the time that this was being made rather too much of. She had never had trouble with her ankles, and she did not see why it would be necessary to give that part of the leg special treatment. What about the knees? Surely they deserved support too; not that they got it, of course. There were many things in this life that deserved support and that did not get it.

Her new boots gave a great deal of ankle support. They were also much lighter than she had imagined. *I could dance in these boots,* she thought.

Oh, so you're thinking of dancing, Boss? You never danced in us.

She glanced into the bag in which she was carrying her old shoes. She was never sure whether her shoes really talked—she thought that it was highly unlikely—and yet they did seem to make remarks from time to time. Usually their comments were of a reproachful or critical nature; shoes, it seemed, were rather resentful, put-upon things that clearly did not accept their manifest destiny underfoot.

Don't worry about them, Boss. It was a different voice. The new shoes spoke in a firm, confident tone. She looked down at them.

That's right, Boss. You trust in us. We know where we're going.

That, she thought, was exactly what one would want to hear of boots. It did not matter so much with ordinary town shoes, but it mattered a great deal with boots. If one were going into danger—and the Okavango Delta was filled with wild animals—then it would undoubtedly be a good thing to have shoes that could look after themselves in difficult conditions.

That's us, Boss! said the boots. *That's us, all right.*

She continued walking, coming to the end of Odi Drive and turning onto Maratadiba Road. There were deserted houses on that corner—old buildings now half eaten by termites, half covered in the bush that grows so quickly over human efforts. It was a good place for snakes, she thought; even here in the city, in these forgotten corners of wasteland, snakes might make their homes: cobras, puff adders, even mambas. She glanced at the tangle of vegetation that had been brought by the recent rains. Everything greened so quickly, transformed from thinness and brownness, thickened, ran riot. She gazed at the derelict windows, their glass broken; at the bulging walls that would surely soon collapse. Yes, there were snakes there, but she had these boots, and that was exactly what boots were for.

She stopped. She looked behind her, back in the direction of Tlokweng. The radio had spoken of rain, and the sky confirmed the forecast. A bank of purple cloud had built up to the east, and even as she had been walking from the shops it had grown in size and anger. Now it filled half the sky; to the west it was light and sunny, to the east it was storms and rain. It happened so quickly, the clouds sweeping in within minutes. And with them was that smell of rain, that half dusty smell that was like no other, over-powering in the intensity of its associations for anyone raised in a dry country. It was synonymous with joy, with renewal, with life itself.

Pula, she muttered; a word that stood for so much, that meant joy, and money, and rain. And rain it was, with initial, fat drops falling on the dusty ground to make a tiny crater in the sand; and then another million such craters before the ground became a shimmer of water. It was so sudden, and she looked around as the water began to stream down her face. It was in her eyes; warm and welcome, but to be wiped away so that she could see through the watery curtain of white that was all about her.

The only place to shelter was one of the deserted houses, almost obscured now in the torrent of the storm. She ran, her boots making her sure-footed in the water and mud. There was a door, which stood ajar, and beyond it a room in which the ceiling boards hung down in fragments. All this work, all this human effort, all brought to this.

With the storm outside, the room was darkened further than what must have been its usual gloom. She looked about her. The concrete floor was shattered here and there, as if by small, localised earthquakes. There was a smell, and there was a person, a man sitting on his haunches at the far end of the room, staring at her. He was an old man, and his face was criss-crossed by lines. She saw his eyes, though, which caught the light, dim though it was, from what had once been the window.

She gave a start. The man smiled. "Do not be afraid, Mma. This is my house, but you are welcome to shelter from the rain."

She took in what was on the floor. A bag from which a few old clothes, rags really, spilled. A few cans, open and abandoned. A single bicycle wheel, salvaged for some reason and then forgotten.

She took a step forward, and then another. She squatted down beside him, remembering this easy, chairless way of sitting that is so natural in Africa.

"I come from up there," the old man said, pointing north.

She nodded. He spoke Setswana in the accent of an age ago.

"So this is your house," she said. "I always thought that there was nobody here."

"There is always somebody," he said.

Mma Makutsi looked up at the failed ceiling. The drumming of the rain on the roof was less insistent now. She would be able to continue her walk soon. She reached into the pocket of her blouse. She had a fifty-pula note in it, now damp from the rain. She gave it to the man, and he took it, examining it carefully as one might examine an important document.

"Thank you, Mma. You do not have to pay to visit my house, though."

"This is a present, Rra. It is not payment."

He put the note away, somewhere in the rags that were his clothes. Then they waited, in silence, for the storm to abate and for the sky to appear again. Mma Makutsi rose to her feet and went to look out of the door. There were stretches of water where once there had been red earth. These would drain quickly, as the water percolated deep down into the thirsty heart of Botswana, somewhere far below the Kalahari.

She turned to say goodbye to the man whose house she had visited. He raised a hand and smiled. She thought: This is the first time I have given anybody fifty pula. It felt very strange; very satisfactory.

On the way out, her shoes suddenly addressed her. The boots were silent, having to cope with the challenge of the wet that was all about. But this came from the shoes in the bag, who said, quite clearly, *We saw that, Boss. We were proud.*

CHAPTER TWELVE

THE PRIVATE CHAIR

SHORTLY BEFORE FIVE O'CLOCK, Mma Makutsi left her house in Extension 2 and walked down to the end of the road to catch a minibus. Her destination was Phuti's aunt's house. This aunt lived on a small road off Limpopo Drive, in an area known as Extension 22, on the eastern boundary of the town. Mma Makutsi knew very little about her, and indeed was not sure that she even knew her name; Phuti simply called her Aunty, although sometimes he used the term No. 1 Aunty. Mma Makutsi had seen the house before, as she had once driven past it and Phuti had said, "That place in there is the house of my No. 1 Aunty. That is her car." Mma Makutsi had not liked the look of the car, an old brown vehicle with very small windows; it was not a friendly car, she felt.

The minibus dropped her at the end of Limpopo Drive and she walked the last half a mile or so to the aunt's house. The aunt would not be expecting her, and she was worried about the reception she would get. Phuti had not telephoned, and that worried her, but she had assumed that he had been adjusting to being out of hospital and would get round to phoning in due course.

As she stood in front of the house, noting, with regret, that the unwelcoming brown car was parked prominently before the veranda, she asked herself why she should not visit her fiancé. Even if he was staying with a relative who clearly did not like her, she was his fiancée and she was entitled to see him. She was not going to encourage him to leave the aunt—it was probably a good place for him to stay while he was recovering, as it would be difficult, if he moved to her place, for her to give him her full attention while working. And yet the aunt was jealous, and hostile, and this visit would not be easy.

She opened the gate and began to walk up to the front veranda. There was a mopipi tree in front of the house and a wild fig, a *moumo,* to the side. There were aloes too, in flower: a bed of flaming red planted right up against the house, like a row of angry spears. She remembered that being used as a purgative: her own aunt knew all about the traditional uses of these plants, and would recommend aloe when purging was required. Phuti's aunt might benefit from a dose of aloes, she said to herself, and smiled at the thought.

There was a button to the side of the door with RING HERE written beside it. This was unusual: people did not bother with bells, usually, being content with an old-fashioned knock. She pressed the bell, but no sound came from within. She pressed it again, and then knocked loudly, calling out, *"Ko! Ko!"*

It took a couple of minutes for the door to be opened by the aunt. She was clearly surprised, and for a moment she did not reply to Mma Makutsi's greeting. Then, when she did, her tone was hostile. "I am sorry. You cannot see Phuti. He is sleeping now. I am very sorry that you have had a wasted journey."

Mma Makutsi tried to look over the aunt's shoulder into the room beyond. There was a radio playing somewhere in the background, Radio Botswana. Phuti listened to Radio Botswana—but so did everyone.

"I can wait until he wakes up," said Mma Makutsi.

The aunt pursed her lips. "There is not room for you to wait. I am very sorry."

Mma Makutsi glanced behind her. "I can wait on the veranda, Mma. There is a chair."

The aunt indicated that this would not do. "That is a private chair, Mma. I'm very sorry. We can't have anybody sitting in that chair."

Mma Makutsi drew in her breath. "A private chair?"

The aunt nodded. "That is what I said." She looked at her watch. "It is now time for me to do something else, Mma. I shall tell Phuti that you have called to see him, and I'm sure that he will be very happy to hear that."

Mma Makutsi struggled to control herself. The lenses of the large glasses she wore were beginning to mist up. That did not happen very often, but it was a bad sign when it did.

"But I am his fiancée, Mma," she said. "We are engaged to be married, as I think you know."

The aunt stared at her. Mma Makutsi found it difficult to read the emotion in the other woman's gaze. Was it hatred? It did not look quite like it. And then she realised: this was fear. It was just as Mma Ramotswe had said.

"So I think that I have the right to see him. I really think that, Mma. Not some time in the future, but now-now." It was a bold statement, and she felt her heart pounding within her as she spoke.

The aunt shifted slightly on her feet. "You say you are engaged, Mma. That is very interesting. I do not recall any *lobola* being agreed, or maybe my memory is going. I do not think that this family has agreed to pay any *lobola* to . . ."—she paused, looking squarely at Mma Makutsi—"to any other *family*."

Mma Makutsi recoiled at the way she said *family*, dwelling on the word, filling it with contempt. Mma Makutsi was not the only one being insulted here; this was an insult to her people in Bobonong, to her uncles; to the uncle with the broken nose, to the uncle who experienced difficulty in finding the right word.

The aunt now continued. "You are a secretary, I hear, Mma."

"Assistant detective."

The aunt laughed. "So that is the new word for secretary. They are always inventing new words for old things. So that is what they call a secretary today—an assistant detective." She was enjoying herself, and stopped to relish her own words. "And what do they call a cook these days, I wonder? Is he also a detective, do you think? Or do they call him a pilot, or a general? What do you think, Mma?"

Mma Makutsi felt flustered. "I am not talking about any of that," she said. And then the response came to her. "Actually, I do not know what they call a cook, Mma. But I do know what they call an aunt who has only bitterness in her heart. They call her a cow. That is what they call her."

She turned on her heel and left the veranda. As she passed the unfriendly brown car, with its small, mean-spirited windows, she heard the aunt shouting behind her. But she was not going to stop; she had seen enough village shouting-matches up in Bobonong to know that the thing to do was to walk away. Phuti would not get her message, she suspected, but the aunt could not detain him forever. He would run away if she tried. Or hop, she thought, bitterly; the aunt might take his new leg and hide it and he would have to hop. She did not like to think about it.

SHE WENT STRAIGHT from the aunt's house to Mma Ramotswe's house on Zebra Drive. She did not like to trouble Mma
Ramotswe at home, and rarely did so, but there were times when
only the company of her employer, that wise, good woman, would
do. This, she felt, was such an occasion, and she knew that Mma
Ramotswe would understand.

She found her on the veranda, as she had hoped she would,
drinking a cup of red bush tea.

"I have just come back," said Mma Ramotswe. "I had a long
talk with Herbert Mateleke. Now I need some tea to recover."
She indicated for Mma Makutsi to sit down.

"So this chair is not a private chair," said Mma Makutsi, as
she lowered herself into it.

"What?" asked Mma Ramotswe. "What is this about private
chairs?"

Mma Makutsi explained that she had been to see Phuti, and
had been denied the opportunity to sit on the veranda and wait.
"There was a chair there," she said. "But the aunt said that it was
a private chair."

Mma Ramotswe let out a hoot of laughter. "A private chair?
What a silly thing to say! Can I give you some tea, Mma, in one of
my private cups? Or perhaps they are not private. Perhaps they
are public."

Mma Makutsi grinned. The encounter with the aunt had
been traumatic, but now Mma Ramotswe was reminding her that
it was really rather ridiculous. "And then I called her a cow. And I
walked away."

Again Mma Ramotswe laughed. "If she is a cow, then she is a
very thin cow," she said. "Perhaps she will get fatter now that the

rains have arrived and there is more grass. I hope that Phuti finds good grazing for her." She was smiling, but then she stopped. "It is funny, but maybe we shouldn't laugh too much, Mma. She is a poor, unhappy woman."

"She is stopping me from seeing Phuti."

"Then phone him. He has a mobile phone, doesn't he?"

Mma Makutsi explained that she had tried to do so, but that she had not got through. "I think that the battery is flat," she said. "He was always forgetting to charge it, and I do not think he has been able to do that since he was in hospital." She thought of other possibilities. "Maybe he has lost the phone, or it was stolen in hospital. There are always thieves in those places."

Mma Ramotswe looked thoughtful. What Mma Makutsi said about thieves in hospitals was quite true. Recently she had heard of a thief who had become ill and had to spend a couple of weeks in hospital. He not only stole food and money from other patients in his ward, but he took the soap from the bathrooms and several bottles of aspirin from the nurses' cupboard. Finally he lifted a stethoscope from the pocket of the doctor attending him and was caught trying to sell it to another doctor.

"Whatever has happened," said Mma Ramotswe, "you know that sooner or later Phuti will be in touch. He will telephone. He will send a message. He's not going to ignore you, is he?"

Mma Makutsi knew that this was probably true, but she was worried that the aunt would try to prevent him from getting in touch. She had shown her cards, and they did not favour Mma Makutsi.

"It's very unfair, Mma. It really is. That woman has kidnapped him—that's what she's done."

Mma Ramotswe took Mma Makutsi's arm and patted it reassuringly. "I don't think it's kidnapping, Mma. He's an adult, and he must have gone with her of his own free will. That is not kidnapping, Mma." She searched her assistant's face and found only anxiety.

"Listen, Mma," Mma Ramotswe went on. "You need to take your mind off all this. We are going to go up to Maun, and, if you like, we can go up a day or two early. Then, when we come back to Gaborone, I'm sure that Phuti will be ready to see you. There will be a message, I'm sure there will."

Mma Makutsi was not entirely persuaded, but she felt calmer now. Talking to Mma Ramotswe had that effect, she had noticed: everybody felt calmer when they had discussed things with her. It did not have to be anything important—although Mma Ramotswe was always willing to talk about weighty matters—you could talk to her about something as simple as the weather or the price of sausages, and you would come away reassured. Perhaps the weather was not going to be as dry and hot as everybody feared—perhaps there really would be good rains; perhaps sausages were not as expensive as they appeared to be, given that they contained all that meat, and there was no wastage with a sausage.

"A day or two early, Mma?" she asked. "When . . ."

"The day after tomorrow," said Mma Ramotswe impulsively. She had a case to work on the next day, but after that she would be free. "We now have our boots, don't we? Then we are ready. All you need to do, Mma, is to pack a small bag of clothes and we can go."

Mma Makutsi closed her eyes. She felt a delicious anticipation. Maun, she thought. The day after tomorrow! *And here, ladies and gentlemen, we have Mma Makutsi, Dip. Sec., Chief Detective at the No. 1 Ladies' Detective Agency, photographed recently while working on an important investigation in the Delta. Mma Makutsi is wearing a pair of special safari boots purchased from a high-class retailer in Gaborone. The traditionally built lady at the back of the photograph is Mma Makutsi's assistant and secretary, Precious Ramotswe . . .*

She opened her eyes. Mma Ramotswe was looking at her with curiosity. She could not have read my mind, Mma Makutsi thought, dispelling a pang of guilt over the fantasy. Of course not . . .

But her shoes had known what she was thinking. *Fat chance, Boss,* they suddenly said. *In your dreams!*

CHAPTER THIRTEEN

MR. JOE BOSILONG, LLB, ATTORNEY

THE CASE that Mma Ramotswe had to deal with before leaving for Maun was that of Mr. Kereleng. She had been putting it off because she was convinced that it was hopeless, but now that she had sorted out the Mateleke inquiry she felt that she had no excuse for ignoring this tricky Kereleng–Sephotho matter. And tackle it she did the following morning, when she went to see her old friend Joe Bosilong, an attorney who had acted for her in one or two disputes over unpaid bills. He had won these disputes not because of any great forensic skills on his part, but because Mma Ramotswe's case was so strong. But she gave him the credit for this, calling him, to his evident amusement and pleasure, the finest attorney south of the Limpopo River.

"So it's Mma Ramotswe," he said heartily as she came into his waiting room in the modest office building near the Private Hospital. "Is this a business call or a social one? Both are equally welcome—from you."

She greeted him warmly. "It is a call for advice. Not for me, you'll understand, but for one of my clients."

"Your friends are my friends," said Mr. Bosilong. "Your clients are my clients. Or maybe not, but you know what I mean. Come in, Mma Ramotswe."

He led her into the office beyond the waiting room. His desk, unusually for a lawyer, was devoid of papers. On the wall behind him, neatly shelved, was a set of the Botswana Law Reports and the Statutes of Botswana. He noticed her looking at them. "So many laws," he said, shaking his head. "Our legislators sit there dreaming up so many laws. It's difficult enough getting on top of them as a lawyer—imagine what it's like for an ordinary person. How can an ordinary person know what the law is?"

"It is very hard," said Mma Ramotswe. "I'm an ordinary person, and I can assure you, it's very hard. Mind you, I think that most people know whether or not they're doing wrong."

"In some cases, perhaps. But there are lots of ways you can break the law without knowing that you're doing so. And ignorance of the law is no excuse, as Professor Frimpong taught me at law school all those years ago."

Mma Ramotswe nodded. "So I believe." She knew that Mr. Bosilong liked to talk at great length about anything, and she would have to move the conversation on if she was to get the advice she wanted.

"Tell me, Rra," she said. "If I buy a house and I put it in the name of another person, and I then change my mind, is there anything I can do?"

Mr. Bosilong frowned. "You've bought a house, have you, Mma Ramotswe? What about Zebra Drive?"

"Not me," she said. "Remember, I told you that this question was for a client. I have a client, you see, who bought a house and put it in the name of—"

She was about to say "in the name of Violet Sephotho," but the lawyer beat her to it. "Violet Sephotho."

Mma Ramotswe's eyes widened. Gaborone was a small town

in many ways, and people talked. It was perhaps not all that surprising that he should have heard of this. "You have heard of this, Rra?"

Mr. Bosilong hesitated. "You put me in a very awkward position, Mma. I am not sure what to say. Indeed, I'm not sure if I should say anything at all."

She looked at him quizzically. And then it dawned on her: he had acted for Violet Sephotho, or possibly for Mr. Kereleng. Again, this should not have surprised her. There were only so many lawyers in Gaborone, and only so many clients; the odds that he should have acted for either of them were small enough. Yet that gave rise to an immediate problem: as an attorney, he was bound by the rules of confidentiality, and he would therefore not be able to say anything about the matter.

"I do not want you to break a confidence, Rra," she said. "I am a detective, and I understand professional confidentiality."

The lawyer sighed. "Oh dear, Mma Ramotswe. This is very difficult. I have acted for this man, Kereleng. When he bought the house initially, it was in his name. Then he came to see me about some other problem he had—a problem with the manager of his bottle store—and he asked me about transferring the house to his fiancée. She is called Violet Sephotho, as you may know. I told him that there would be no problem about that. Then the fiancée came to see me and asked me to draw up the deed for him to sign. When I did that, I was acting for her, not for him. She was my client. That's important, you know."

Mma Ramotswe looked puzzled. "Why? What difference does it make?"

"Well," said Mr. Bosilong, "she was my client, you see, and that meant I owed a duty to her. So when Mr. Kereleng came to see me later and said that he had changed his mind, I had to tell him that it was too late. He was not the client—she was. He asked me to give the deed back—it had not yet been sent to the land registry. I said I could not, as I had done that job for another client, Miss Sephotho."

Mma Ramotswe was interested in one thing he had said. "You told me that the deed was not yet registered. Is that so?"

"Not yet," he said. "I suppose I've been putting it off." He paused, looking into Mma Ramotswe's eyes. "Mma Ramotswe, can I trust you?"

"Of course you can, Rra."

"No, I mean absolutely, completely trust you. One hundred per cent?"

"One hundred per cent, Rra. Anything you say to me will go no further."

Mr. Bosilong looked about him, as if searching his office for eavesdroppers.

"What I am about to say must remain between us," he said. "I think that this Miss Sephotho is dishonest. I think that she has prevailed on this man to give her this house pretending that she will marry him. But it is only a pretence."

Mma Ramotswe laughed. "But I knew that all along, Rra. Everybody knows that—or just about everybody. Mr. Kereleng didn't at first—now he does."

Mr. Bosilong shook his head ruefully. "I am an honest man, Mma Ramotswe. I cannot abide wicked people."

"None of us can," she said.

"And it makes me very sad when I see a legal technicality allowing bad people to get away with it."

"There is nothing worse than that," she agreed, "because that means that not only does the wicked person get away with it, but people lose respect for the law of Botswana. That is not a good thing at all."

Mr. Bosilong signalled that this was his feeling too. But then he said, "Of course, sometimes things go wrong in the law. Attorneys make mistakes. They file the wrong papers. They forget to do things."

"Every one of us makes mistakes, Rra," said Mma Ramotswe. She was not sure exactly what he was going to propose, but she wanted to encourage him. "And sometimes," she went on, "a mistake is for the best." She hesitated. "In fact, sometimes it is best to make an intentional mistake . . ."

Her words clearly brought him relief. "That is good to hear. You see . . ." His voice tailed off.

She spoke gently. "See what, Rra?"

"You see, I have made a mistake in that deed. I did not mean to make it, but I made it. I described the plot of land incorrectly. I put in the number of the neighbouring plot, and it is also the neighbouring plot in the land map that accompanies the deed. I was careless."

A smile broke out on Mma Ramotswe's face. "So Mr. Kereleng signed a deed that transferred his neighbour's house rather than his?"

"I'm afraid so. Which makes me look very foolish."

"And you didn't tell him?"

Mr. Bosilong stared down at his desk. "Everything was done through her. I had my instructions from her. I should have advised him to get independent legal advice. I did not. It would not look good for me if there was a complaint."

"So it's a mess?"

"It's a mess, Mma."

But she did not think it was. "Tell me, Rra: If you took that deed to the land registry, what would happen?"

"It would be null and void. They would check it, and they

would see the mistake. They would see that Mr. Kereleng does not have title to pass on the property in the deed. They would throw it out."

"So you need to tell Violet Sephotho that the thing you did for her has not been done properly."

"I will look very stupid."

Mma Ramotswe rose to her feet. "You are not stupid, Rra. You have saved a man from being very badly treated. Your mistake was a good mistake. It was the best mistake I have heard of for a long time."

"I cannot bring myself to tell her that the deed is void and that she must get out. It's not easy, Mma."

Mma Ramotswe understood. But there was a way round this, she thought, and so she suggested that Mr. Bosilong type out an amendment to be signed by Mr. Kereleng. Of course he would not sign it, but at least it would make the situation easier for Mr. Bosilong. She would go to see Violet on his behalf. She was quite happy to do that.

The lawyer listened to the suggestion. Slowly he began to smile. "It *does* make it easier, Mma. It really does. I am not a coward—normally—but now I am in a very big mess, and you have made it so much easier for me."

"Then type it out right now, Rra," she said. "Then I shall go and give it to Violet Sephotho."

"He will never sign it," said Mr. Bosilong.

"Of course he won't," said Mma Ramotswe. "That's the whole idea."

"You are very clever, Mma," said Mr. Bosilong.

Mma Ramotswe shook her head. "I am not a clever lady," she said. "I am an ordinary lady."

Mr. Bosilong would have none of this. "No," he said. "You are clever. Lawyers think they are clever, but then they are not."

Mma Ramotswe was not sure whether he expected her to refute this, but she did not, and the subject of who was clever and who was not was left where it was.

SHE WAITED until after five o'clock before she went to Violet's house, or, as she reminded herself—with some satisfaction— Mr. Kereleng's house. The afternoon passed slowly, as there was little happening in the office. At first Mma Ramotswe had decided not to tell Mma Makutsi of her visit that morning to Joe Bosilong because she was concerned that her assistant would find it difficult to be professionally detached from any case involving Violet Sephotho. As the day wore on, however, she found it increasingly difficult not to tell her the good news that she had discovered for Mr. Kereleng. Eventually she succumbed to the temptation, and told Mma Makutsi about her visit to the lawyer and his extraordinary disclosure.

As she had anticipated, Mma Makutsi was ecstatic. "That is very, very exciting news, Mma. I am so pleased for poor Mr. Kereleng."

Mma Ramotswe watched her. Yes, Mma Makutsi was pleased for Mr. Kereleng, but she was undoubtedly much more pleased at the foiling of Violet Sephotho's plans. And Mma Makutsi's next remark confirmed that. "There are some ladies who deserve to be exposed," she said. "Violet Sephotho is number one on the list. In fact, she is the only one on the list. I cannot wait to see her face when we tell her. Oh, I cannot wait, Mma! It is the best thing ever!"

Mma Ramotswe held up a hand. "I don't think that we should make too much of a fuss, Mma. I was just going to slip over there after five, when she should be back from work. I will simply tell her that the deed is invalid and needs to be signed again. Of course she'll know that Mr. Kereleng won't sign, so she'll know that her little trick has not worked."

"Little trick?" exclaimed Mma Makutsi. "Mma, it is not a little trick—it is a great big theft! No, she must be fully exposed. She must be shown for what she is. She must be made to crawl in the dust, Mma. In the dust."

Mma Ramotswe understood the passion behind all this. After all, Violet Sephotho had tried to seduce Phuti Radiphuti away from Mma Makutsi, and it was understandable that she should feel aggrieved. But Mma Ramotswe was not a vindictive woman, and she did not relish the humiliation of anybody, no matter how deserving of such treatment.

"It is not a good idea to make anybody crawl," she said mildly. "Either in the dust or anywhere else. I do not think we need to do that, Mma."

Mma Makutsi appeared to take the reproach well. "I am very angry with her, Mma. I did not mean that I wanted to see her crawl in the dust—not really. I just wanted her to know that she cannot get away with such things. That is all." She waited a moment, and then continued, "And I shall not say anything when we go to see her. I promise you that, Mma. I shall be silent, and in the background."

Mma Ramotswe realised that her assistant would be gravely upset if she were to be prevented from accompanying her on the visit to Violet Sephotho, and so she agreed, reluctantly, that she could come. "But remember, Mma," she warned. "I shall do the talking."

"I shall remember that," said Mma Makutsi and then, privately—but spotted by Mma Ramotswe—she closed her eyes in utterly pleasurable anticipation.

SO!" said Violet Sephotho. "So, this is a very big surprise for me. Two famous detectives on my doorstep. What an honour!"

"I hope you are well, Mma," said Mma Ramotswe. "And I hope you will invite us in."

Violet Sephotho's eyes grew wide. "Of course, of course," she said coquettishly. "We cannot have Mma Ramotswe and . . ." She knew Mma Makutsi's name, of course; she knew it well, as they had studied together at the Botswana Secretarial College, but it suited her to seem to forget. "And . . ."

"Grace Makutsi," hissed Mma Makutsi. "You remember me."

Mma Ramotswe threw a warning glance at her assistant.

"Of course," said Violet. "Grace Makutsi. The Botswana Secretarial College. Sorry to have forgotten, but some people are hard to remember. Anyway, please both come in."

They stepped into the front room of the house, a living room that doubled up as a dining room. The room had been recently painted, and there were several framed prints on the wall. There was a picture of the Eiffel Tower and one of New York.

"That is Paris," said Violet. "And that is New York. You have heard of these places?"

"I have heard of them," said Mma Ramotswe.

"And you, Grace?" asked Violet.

"I have heard of them too," said Mma Makutsi through tightened lips.

"And then there is Johannesburg," said Violet airily. "That is such an exciting city, and it's not so far away. I will be going there next weekend, I think. Four hours by car."

"It is very easy to get to Johannesburg," said Mma Ramotswe pleasantly. "My father used to work in the mines there in the days when all the men went off to South Africa for work. Things are so different now."

"Oh yes," said Violet. "There are many different things today.

I am always finding different things." She looked at her visitors and smiled. Mma Ramotswe noticed that she had applied thick purple eyeliner in copious quantities.

Violet looked at her watch. "I'm sorry, Bomma, that I cannot give you tea or anything. But I am going out tonight. There is a big dance at the Grand Palm. I am going there. By invitation." She paused. "And maybe you will tell me why you have come to see me?"

There was something in her tone that suggested she was on edge. She knows there is something wrong, thought Mma Ramotswe. And for a minute she felt sympathy for this ruthless, ambitious woman. She knew.

"I am a messenger today," said Mma Ramotswe. "I sometimes do that sort of thing."

"Not enough detective work?" asked Violet, her confidence momentarily returning.

"I do things for friends," said Mma Ramotswe. "I am a friend of a certain lawyer. He is called Joe Bosilong."

Violet was quite still. One of her heavily purpled eyelids moved slightly; the smallest tic. "I know him," she said. "He is my lawyer."

"Yes," said Mma Ramotswe. "He has sent me with an amendment to the deed he drew up for you recently. There is a mistake in it. It will have to be signed again by that kind man who is giving you this house, Mr. Kereleng."

Violet said nothing.

Then Mma Makutsi spoke. "Unless he won't sign, of course."

Violet spun round to face her. "You said something, Mma?" she said, her voice rising to a high pitch.

"I said that maybe Mr. Kereleng won't sign. And if that happens, then I'm afraid that he will be taking this house back."

"Mma Makutsi—," Mma Ramotswe began. But she could

not continue. Violet Sephotho, screaming, had launched herself into an attack on Mma Makutsi. It happened so quickly that Mma Ramotswe had little time to think about her reaction. Moving forward, she caught hold of Violet's flailing arms and brought them to her sides. It was the first time in her entire career as a detective that she had used force. It shocked her.

"Get out of my house, Grace Makutsi!" screamed the now physically restrained Violet. "You get out! You, *voetsek, voetsek!*"

Mma Makutsi was calm. "You have too much purple on your eyelids," she said. "Purple Sephotho!" And then, as she and Mma Ramotswe retreated from the room, Mma Makutsi threw her parting shot over her shoulder, "Fifty per cent!"

Outside, Mma Ramotswe found her breath coming in short bursts. "Are you all right, Mma?" asked Mma Makutsi.

"I am very upset," said Mma Ramotswe, stopping to get her breath back. "That was a very nasty scene."

"She is a nasty woman," said Mma Makutsi. "That purple eyeliner, I . . ."

"Do not talk about that, Mma," said Mma Ramotswe.

"She is a horrible . . ."

"Yes," said Mma Ramotswe simply. She felt herself shaking. "She is unhappy, and she brings unhappiness to others. That is very sad. I am sorry for her."

Mma Makutsi looked up at the sky. How could Mma Ramotswe even begin to have sympathy for that terrible woman? How could she? And then, suddenly, she remembered how. It was because this woman, this traditionally built woman, this understanding, tolerant employer, this detective, was composed of kindness, just of kindness.

"I'm sorry," said Mma Makutsi. "I did not behave very well in there."

Mma Ramotswe took her hand. "You were a bit excited,

maybe. But you didn't do too badly. When she attacked you, you did nothing, which was the right thing to do." Suddenly she laughed. "That eyeliner!" she said. "What a colour!"

"I can't wait to tell Phuti about this," said Mma Makutsi.

There was a silence, which Mma Ramotswe tried to fill. "I'm sure that you will see him soon," she said. "Then you can tell him."

She was not sure, though. She had a bad feeling about that aunt of Phuti's. That was the problem, she thought. You deal with one difficult person in this life—Violet Sephotho, for instance—and another one pops up.

But for a short while she could put such difficulties aside. Now she had the pleasant duty of going to tell Mr. Kereleng that he had his house back; it had never really been Violet's anyway, thanks to the faulty deed, but now he could go and claim it back, and then sell it to raise the money for his laboratory. There were so many things in this world that did not turn out well; she was glad that here, at least, was one that had turned out very well indeed.

She went to his office. He was embarrassed at first, and explained to her in a lowered voice that they were not meant to receive personal callers at work. But when she told him what had happened, his demeanour changed. He let out a whoop of delight, and then began to cry. His colleagues watched in amazement, and then one came over to Mma Ramotswe and asked her if Mr. Kereleng had received bad news. "No," she said. "It is very good news. Sometimes people cry if they are very happy, or very relieved."

"That is very odd," said the colleague.

"No, it is not," said Mma Ramotswe. "We should all cry a bit more, Rra. We really should."

CHAPTER FOURTEEN

INTO THE DELTA

THE DRIVE NORTH took longer than they had expected. In spite of their early start, the road was busy for the first part of the journey, with large stock carriers occupying both lanes and inconsiderately making it difficult to pass. In the days of the tiny white van that would have been neither here nor there—that van had been unable to pass anything much, although it usually managed to get past bicycles, and pedestrians, if conditions were right. The new blue van, of course, experienced no such difficulties, having reserves of power deep in its engine that Mma Ramotswe could release with a simple movement of her right foot. That ability, though, was such a novelty that she hardly dared use it. What would happen, she wondered, if she put her foot down hard to the floor and left it there? She had done that frequently enough in the old van, and there was rarely any reaction. It was as if that engine did not receive its instructions, or, if it did, it merely shrugged them off, as an aged beast of burden, a donkey or an ox, may ignore its owner's exhortations, saying, effectively, *I am just too old to be doing this any more. Leave me alone please.*

Mma Makutsi proved to be a helpful companion and co-driver. She did not possess a driving licence—not yet—but she took the view that the obtaining of ninety-seven per cent in the final examinations of the Botswana Secretarial College, if not amounting to an actual driving qualification, entitled her to hold views and to advise. So she kept a lookout when Mma Ramotswe wanted to pass something. *Now, Mma, right now. Just go a bit faster. There is nothing coming. Go now.* She also navigated—which was not an exacting task given that the road to Francistown, which marked the end of the first leg of the journey, ran straight and true from Gaborone northwards and neither meandered nor diverted. "You go straight here, Mma," said Mma Makutsi. "That sign over there says Francistown. That is the route to take." Mma Ramotswe nodded. "Yes," she said. "These are good signs, don't you think, Mma? They make it quite clear which way you should go."

Mma Makutsi, interpreting this as veiled criticism of her navigating, searched for an objection to this remark. "But what if there is a blind person?" she challenged. "What use would they be then?"

"But a blind person shouldn't be driving," said Mma Ramotswe. And added, as if the matter required further resolution, "That is well known, Mma."

There could be no answer to that, and the subject of signs was pursued no further. There were other things to talk about, though, and as their conversation wandered this way and that the long miles clocked up. Towns passed, some well known—Mahalapye and Palapye—some small and unimportant to all except those who lived in them, for whom they were everything. Each had associations or memories for Mma Ramotswe, and, to a lesser extent, for Mma Makutsi. One of them would know somebody who came from there, or had relatives there; one of them would know a story that came from that place—a story of envy or overreaching ambition or simple human need.

"That place," said Mma Makutsi as they drove past a small settlement called Serule. "That is the place where they have discovered uranium. I read about it in the *Botswana Daily News*. They are going to mine it some day. And then those people living in Serule will have a lot of uranium."

"I do not want to have any uranium," said Mma Ramotswe. "They are welcome to it."

"Of course they won't keep it. You do not need to keep uranium."

"There are other things that have happened there," said Mma Ramotswe. "Apart from finding uranium. I knew a man who came from Serule. He had a sister who did very well at school. High marks . . . like yours, Mma."

The compliment pleased Mma Makutsi. She liked people to refer to her results, even if she tried to wear the ninety-seven per cent gracefully. "I see," she said demurely. "And then?"

"The sister was a clever girl. So it was not just hard work. Some people get good results from working very hard, others from being very bright. These people do not have to work very much—they just get their good results. It's like standing under a tree and waiting for the figs to fall into your arms."

At first Mma Makutsi was silent. She was not sure if there was a barb in this remark. But she would let it pass anyway. "Standing under a fig tree is safe enough, Mma," she said. "But you should never stand under a sausage tree." The sausage tree, the *moporoto* in Setswana, was a sort of jacaranda that had heavy fruit like great, pendulous sausages.

"Certainly not, Mma. There are many people who are late now because of that. Those are very heavy pods, and if you get one on your head, then you are in great danger of becoming late."

She used the expression that the Batswana preferred: to become late. There was human sympathy here; to be dead is to be nothing, to be finished. The expression is far too final, too disruptive of the bonds that bind us to one another, bonds that survive the demise of one person. A late father is still your father, even though he is not there; a dead father sounds as if he has nothing further to do—he is finished.

"This girl," Mma Ramotswe continued, "was always doing well. People said, *That girl is going to be an important somebody one day. She will be going to Gaborone, definite.*"

Mma Makutsi frowned. She could tell which way this story was going, as it was an old story in Botswana, a theme repeated time and time again. The person who does well, who excels, is asking for trouble. "People were watching?" asked Mma Makutsi.

Mma Ramotswe confirmed the worst. "They were watching, Mma. They were listening too. There are always people who are watching and listening."

Of course there are, thought Mma Makutsi. She had gone from Bobonong to Gaborone. She knew all about envy.

"Somebody—and they did not know who it was at first—put a spell on this girl."

There was silence. To report the casting of a spell does not mean that you believe in the efficacy of spells. But spells were used, whether or not the rest of us believed in them; and somebody was prepared to believe in them. If that somebody were the victim, then the spell had worked. It was as simple as that. And people could be frightened to death by the knowledge that there was a spell on them; it happened regularly.

"How did she know?" asked Mma Makutsi.

Mma Ramotswe shrugged. "It is difficult to say. Spells are

nothing—they don't exist. So how do you tell when there is nothing there—just air? Maybe somebody spoke to her. That is how people come to know about spells. People say, *They have bought some bad medicine to use against you.* That sort of thing." She did not like to think about it; that was the old Africa, not the Africa of today, and certainly not the Botswana she knew. And yet it was there; just as it was elsewhere in the world, everywhere, really, where underneath the modern and the rational there ran a dark river of unreason and fear.

"The girl told her family," Mma Ramotswe continued. "They said that they had feared something like this would happen. And they tried to keep her in the house. They did not like her to go anywhere except the school. At nights they all slept in the same room with the girl at the back, so that any person who came into the house would have to step over other sleepers before they came to the one they were looking for.

"The mother went quietly to a witch doctor and bought something to protect the girl. Some useless mixture of ground bones and leaves—they love that sort of thing—made into a paste. She put this on the girl's cheeks, although the girl said that she did not believe in this nonsense. The mother said, 'And when something bad happens, will you not believe in it then?' And the girl said, 'All of this is part of a world that has gone now. It is no longer true, any of this.'"

Mma Makutsi shook her head. "Poor girl."

"Yes," said Mma Ramotswe. "Because something bad did happen. She had an old aunt, this girl. Her parents said to her, 'Do not visit your aunt now. Her place is far away. You will be in danger if you go.'

"The girl said that this was just superstition. 'I am a strong girl,' she said. 'How can anything like that harm a strong girl in broad daylight?' That is what she said, Mma, which is just the right thing for her to say. If more people said that sort of thing, then all this business could never flourish. It would die when it is out in the sun. It is a business that needs darkness and fear to stay alive."

Their road was now almost deserted. It was lunchtime, and the sun was high in the sky overhead, casting short, vertical shadows. Before them, stretched out to the distant horizon on either side, was acacia-dominated scrub bush—mile upon mile of olive-green trees, like tiny umbrellas erected against the heat of the sun. And through the windows of the van, open to allow a draught of cooling air, came the noise of the cicadas, that high-pitched screeching that provided a constant background of sound for the African bush.

Light made all the difference. Under this midday sky fear and terror seemed very far away, but at night it was easy to imagine the presence of evil and its attendants, even here.

"The girl went to see her aunt. She walked a long way to see her, and then said goodbye to her aunt and began the walk back. It was mid-afternoon. But it was getting dark, because it was the rainy season—as it is now. There was lightning. The girl said later that she knew that she was going to be hit because she could smell the lightning before it came. People say that it has a smell, Mma, but I have never smelled it because I have never been close enough. I do not want to get so close to lightning that I shall be able to smell it—just as I do not want to get close enough to smell a lion's breath.

"She started to run when the rain drew near, but the storm was too quick for her and it caught up with her. That is when she was struck by lightning, thrown to the ground and knocked out. They took her back to her place when they found her. They thought that she was dead because she did not move, not even to breathe, and they could see the burns on her clothes that told them what had happened. Her family wailed and wailed and called the headman to tell him what had happened. He said that it was difficult to go to the police in such cases because they could not tell who had put a spell on the girl. 'And how can anybody prove anything?' he asked. 'This is the doing of lightning. You cannot arrest lightning.'

"That night the girl woke up. They screamed some more when they saw the body move, but they were happy too. The girl told them what had happened. 'I have been dreaming since then,' she said. 'So that is what it is like to be late,' her father said. 'It is as if you are dreaming.'

"The girl's mother had a good idea. She said, 'Let's go ahead with the funeral tomorrow because we have already killed the cow for the guests. But let us see if we can find out who put this spell on our daughter. If she wakes up at the funeral, we shall see who runs away, and we shall know who it is.'

"They all thought that this was a good idea, even the girl. 'It will be very good to be at my own funeral,' she said. 'I shall hear the things that people say about me, and I shall find out who my friends are.' "

Mma Makutsi interrupted Mma Ramotswe at this point. "I am not so sure," she said. "People do not always tell the truth at funerals. They say things that are not true because they feel guilty about the way they have treated the late person. I have seen that happen many times. In fact, if you listened to what was said at funerals, you would think that this is a land of saints."

Mma Ramotswe agreed that this was largely true. "Yes," she said. "That may be true, but people are trying their best, remember. And they may believe what they say."

"All those lies?" asked Mma Makutsi. "They would believe all those lies?"

Mma Ramotswe pointed out that many people came to

believe the lies they told. Politicians, she said, were a bit like that. "They get so used to telling lies that they begin to think that these lies are true. It is very sad."

But that was not the point of the story, she reminded Mma Makutsi. "They all said that they would go ahead with the funeral, and it was also agreed that the girl should jump out of the coffin in the middle of the service and say that there was one present who had put a spell on her, and she knew who this person was. Then everybody was to look for the one who ran away, as surely such a person would run away in such circumstances."

Mma Makutsi could barely wait for the outcome. "They carried her in, Mma? As if she was late?"

"Yes, they did that, Mma. It was all planned. They were going to sing a Setswana hymn—you know that one, 'The Yoke Is Heavy upon Me'—and then the girl was to knock on the coffin. Then they would let her sit up and make her denunciation of the spell that had almost killed her. But there was a problem."

Mma Makutsi drew in her breath. A problem? Perhaps the girl had suffocated and was now really dead. Perhaps she had gone to sleep and had to be woken up by her family. She raised these possibilities with Mma Ramotswe, who said no, it had not been like that. Then what had happened?

"The father said that they should open the coffin and check on the body. The reverend, who did not know about the plan, was surprised, but did not want to upset a man in mourning, and so he agreed. That is when they got a bad shock, Mma Makutsi. A bad, bad shock."

Mma Makutsi covered her face with her hands. "I do not want to hear the end of this story, Mma Ramotswe. I am too frightened."

"It was not the girl in there at all," said Mma Ramotswe.

"They had mixed up the coffins, and the girl had gone to another funeral altogether."

Mma Makutsi let out a scream. "Oh, Mma! That is terrible. They might have already buried the other one."

"Yes, they might have. But fortunately they did not."

Mma Makutsi let out a sigh of relief. "That is a very happy result," she said. "Real life very seldom works out that way."

"Indeed," said Mma Ramotswe. "If we believe that story. I am not sure . . ."

But Mma Makutsi appeared not to have heard. "It must have been very sad for the people at that funeral—the one where the late person started knocking on the coffin. Their hopes must have been raised that the dear brother or sister inside was no longer late. And then, when they discovered that it was another person, they must have been very upset."

"I don't think so," said Mma Ramotswe. "Apparently that other person was a very difficult person who had made everybody's life a misery. When they heard the knocking they were all very sad, I'm told. Then, when they realised it was somebody else, they were very relieved."

Mma Makutsi laughed at this. It was difficult to imagine being glad over the loss of anybody; she would never rejoice in the demise of another, unless, of course . . . A list started to form in her mind. No. 1. Violet Sephotho. No. 2. Phuti's No. 1 Aunty. No. 3 . . . Was there a No. 3? She could not think of anybody. More minor punishments would do for the rest. And she should not make such a list, she told herself; it was unworthy of her, and she should stop. What if something dreadful were to happen either to Violet or to the aunt? She would be racked with guilt, no doubt, feeling that she had caused the misfortune, in spite of the fact that she knew quite well that one could never be the cause of anything unless you actually *did* something. And just thinking about something could never be said to be doing anything.

They needed to talk about something different, and so Mma Makutsi asked after the children. How was Puso doing at school, and was Motholeli still talking about becoming a mechanic?

"He is doing well," said Mma Ramotswe. "He is not very good at writing but his arithmetic is good. His head is full of numbers, I think."

"That is very useful," said Mma Makutsi. "He can be a book-keeper or an accountant."

Mma Ramotswe smiled. It was difficult for her to imagine Puso grown up, and she saw for a moment an accountant in short trousers, a catapult sticking out of his pocket, and in his hand a jam sandwich of the sort that Puso loved to eat. But children changed, as adults did, and the image in her mind became one of a young man in a suit, with shiny shoes and a businesslike look to him. How everybody would have changed by then; how the country would have changed too.

"And Motholeli?" prompted Mma Makutsi.

"I think that she still wants to be a mechanic. Mr. J.L.B. Matekoni talks to her about cars and she is always asking him about gearboxes and such things. There are not many girls who talk about engines, but she is one."

"That will also be a very good thing," said Mma Makutsi. "It means that there will be a Tlokweng Road Speedy Motors even in twenty years' time, when you and Mr. J.L.B. Matekoni are both late."

Mma Ramotswe did a quick calculation in her head. "I do not think that either of us need be late by then, Mma," she said. "We are not that old."

Mma Makutsi looked doubtful. "Maybe not," she admitted, rather reluctantly, thought Mma Ramotswe.

MANY HOURS and many stories later they reached Maun. It was early evening, and they saw in the distance the first lights of the town in the gathering dusk. There was something deeply reassuring about the sight. It was not simply that they were reaching the end of their long journey; the lights were comforting signs of human settlement in a great emptiness. To the south, under a sky that, as the evening approached, became an expanse of red, were the Makadikadi salt pans, a landscape of improbable whiteness that went on for a hundred miles, forever, it seemed, if one stood on their edge, a tiny human. Mma Ramotswe shivered: to stand on the verge of something so great and so empty seemed to be in danger of being swallowed up; she often felt that when she was in the wild places of her country. It would be so easy to become lost, to disappear, to find yourself alone in a wide slice of Africa, reduced to what you really were, a small and vulnerable creature among many other creatures.

The lights drew nearer. Now they were individual dwellings, dotted here and there amid the acacia scrub. A few had fires outside, small flickering points of orange seen through the trees. A truck, a figure, a set of headlights in the darkness; and then Maun itself, with its streets and lit windows, and its frontier air.

Mma Makutsi looked out of her window. "So this is the place," she said. "So this is it."

"Yes," said Mma Ramotswe. "We must find Mr. J.L.B. Matekoni's cousin's place now."

That, as it happened, was not easy. They took directions from a man they saw standing at the side of the street, near one of the hotels. He sent them off into the night in entirely the wrong direction, or so they were told by the next person from whom they obtained guidance. He was more reliable, and they eventually found the house half an hour after they had arrived in the town.

The cousin himself, Mr. H.B.C. Matekoni, was away, but his wife was welcoming. They had young children, who solemnly welcomed the visitors and were then dispatched back to bed. A meal followed and family news was exchanged, with stories of distant cousins and their doings. Mma Makutsi was tired and went to bed in the room that she was to share with Mma Ramotswe. She lay there, on her narrow bed, listening to the low murmur of conversation in the room next door, relishing the novelty of her situation: she was on a business trip, in Maun; she had new boots that she had worn in the car and that were now at the foot of her bed; she could see the night sky outside, through a small window above her head. There were so many stars, in many cases with names, she believed. Did they have African names too, she wondered? It would be good if they did, she decided, if we named the ones over our own heads, because they were ours just as much as they were anybody's. She felt drowsy, her thoughts wandering; night, stars, the moon . . . Had anyone claimed the moon yet? she asked herself. It would be wrong for anybody to claim the moon; it was everybody's, but if it ever belonged to Botswana then it would be well looked after. We would soon have cattle there, she thought . . . and drifted off.

When Mma Ramotswe came into the room, she found Mma Makutsi asleep, one arm hanging down from her bed, her mouth slightly open, the blanket with which she had covered herself having largely slipped off her. Mma Ramotswe gazed at her assistant for a moment; Mma Makutsi looked different, she noticed, without her large glasses; her face had softened. But now it went further than that; it looked vulnerable, as we all may look in sleep. She reached forward and gently pulled the blanket back over the sleeping woman. Mma Makutsi stirred, but only slightly. Mma Ramotswe turned out her torch and placed it on the table beside her bed. There was enough light from the night sky outside—the light of the moon and stars—to make the torch unnecessary.

She slipped into bed and closed her eyes. She was exhausted from the drive, but she did not drop off to sleep immediately. Her mind was on the next day and what it would bring—on the journey they would have to make to Eagle Island Camp. They would travel by boat, possibly by *makoro,* one of the traditional canoes that people still used to get about the Delta. They were cheap and easily manoeuvred: all that was required was the strength of the paddler and the local knowledge to navigate the confusing channels that fingered their way through the watery landscape around Maun. That knowledge was more than a matter of knowing where to go—an important part of navigating was being aware of who else might be using those channels at the same time. If it was another *makoro,* then all was well. If it was a hippo, though, it was a different matter altogether.

She opened her eyes. Would the boatman be able to spot hippos easily enough? What if he missed one, as people sometimes did? There was only one outcome then—there could be no contest between an angry hippo and a frail canoe. The hippo won.

She told herself to stop worrying. It would take a strong hippo to upset a canoe containing both her and Mma Makutsi. The weight of such a canoe would be considerable, and she wondered whether a hippo would have the strength or energy to upset it. No, they would be safe from hippos and . . . crocodiles. She opened her eyes again. She had heard recently of a terrible incident in which a crocodile had seized somebody from a boat. That was very unusual, but it had happened, and it had happened in Botswana, on the Limpopo River. She shuddered. If the crocodile seized Mma Makutsi, would she have the courage to jump in and rescue her? A crocodile would have difficulty in dealing with two substantial ladies at the same time, especially if they were both determined not to be eaten, and resisted, which she was confident would be the case. There was safety in numbers, perhaps. It was when we were alone that we were in the greatest danger—a rule that applied to so many occasions, she thought, not just to those on which we were confronted with hippopotamuses and crocodiles, and other things in—and out—of the water.

THE COUSIN'S WIFE had arranged with a local boatman to pick them up beside the river.

"This is very exciting," said Mma Makutsi, as they stood beneath a large mopani tree, waiting for their *makoro*. "Do you know something, Mma Ramotswe? I have never been in a boat before."

"Well, you will find out what it is like today," said Mma Ramotswe. She paused. "Can you swim, Mma?"

Mma Makutsi shook her head. "I have never learned to swim. Up in Bobonong we didn't really have any water. It's hard to learn how to swim when there is no water."

Mma Ramotswe considered this observation. It was, she thought, incontestably true. It was not surprising that there were not many champion swimmers in Botswana, as only one part of the country—the Delta—had much water.

"I cannot swim either," she said. "Although I was once invited to go swimming in the pool at the Sun Hotel."

"And did you, Mma Ramotswe?" Mma Makutsi tried not to smile at the picture that came into her mind of Mma Ramotswe entering the pool at the hotel and making the water rise to the point of overflowing. She had been taught about such things at school. She remembered the lesson: "If you place a (large) body in water, the level of the water rises as the body displaces a volume of water equal to the volume of the body."

Mma Ramotswe herself smiled at the recollection. "I went in at the shallow end," she said. "It was not very deep, and I found that I could stand. But then I made a very interesting discovery."

"That you could swim?"

Mma Ramotswe shook her head. "No, I did not find that I could swim. I found, though, that I could float. I very slowly took the weight off my legs, and do you know, Mma, I floated. It was very pleasant. I did not have to move my arms—I just floated."

Mma Makutsi clapped her hands. "That is very good, Mma! Well done! Perhaps it is something to do with being so traditionally built. A thin person would sink. You floated."

"Possibly," said Mma Ramotswe. "But it was good to discover that I could do a sport after all."

Mma Makutsi was not certain that floating could be called a sport. Was there a Botswana floating team? She thought not. What would such a team do? Would they have to float gently from one point to another, with the winner being the one who arrived first? Surely not.

This conversation might have continued had they not then seen the boatman arriving. He came round a bend in the river, standing in his long, narrow canoe, using a pole to propel it forward. Seeing the two women under the tree, he raised a hand in greeting.

Mma Makutsi frowned. "Will we both fit in that, Mma? What if a hippo . . ."

Mma Ramotswe put a finger to her lips. "Let's not talk about hippos, Mma. It is not a good idea to talk about hippos when you are just about to set off on a river journey."

The boatman drew up at the bank in front of them, skilfully beaching the canoe at their feet. They noticed that he had attached a small outboard engine to the back of the *makoro,* and as they placed their overnight bags in the front of the canoe, he whipped the engine into life.

"Eagle Island is too far away for us to be traditional," he said with a smile. "Now that you're paying, I'll turn the engine on."

The two women settled themselves into their places in the canoe. As she did so, Mma Ramotswe noticed the clearance between the top edge of the boat and the surface of the water diminish alarmingly. And that was before Mma Makutsi had sat down. Hippos, she reminded herself, but did not give voice to the thought.

Mma Makutsi lowered herself. "The water is very close," she said to the boatman. "Is that normal?"

The boatman replied in a matter-of-fact tone, "It is not normal, Mma. This canoe is very heavy now. That is why the water is almost coming over the side. But we will be perfectly safe, as long as you two ladies don't move."

Mma Makutsi froze. "And if we do move?" she whispered.

The boatman laughed. "If you move, we could go into the water. Big splash, Mma."

"It isn't funny," said Mma Makutsi, raising her voice. "We are two ladies here on business. We cannot go into the water, where there are . . ."

"Hippos," said the boatman, maintaining his matter-of-fact tone. "And many crocodiles too. And of course sometimes there are also elephants who like to swim in this river. And snakes too. There are snakes who live in the reeds by the side of the river. They like to swim too, Mma. Did you know that?"

"I do not want to hear about these things, Rra," said Mma Makutsi.

Mma Ramotswe decided to say something to allay her assistant's fear. There was no point in Mma Makutsi's spending the trip in a state of terror. She would be cheerful. "Of course you aren't frightened by any of these creatures, are you, Rra?"

The boatman stared at her. "Oh no, I am very frightened, Mma. I would not like to meet a hippo. They are very bad-tempered animals, and they can snap a man in two with those great teeth of theirs. Just like that. Ow! Snap, and he's broken in two."

Mma Ramotswe laughed nervously. "That is very unlikely to happen, Rra," she said.

"Oh, no it isn't, Mma. It happens all the time. It happened two weeks ago. I knew the man who was snapped in two by a hippo. He is—he was—the cousin of my wife's sister's husband. He was a very close relative, and now he is late."

Mma Makutsi looked steadfastly ahead. They had now started their journey, and the *makoro* was heading upstream, throwing out a wake of crystal-clear water on either side of its narrow prow. The water glistened in the sun like a layer of liquid diamonds; beneath, some feet below, lay a clear sand-bank, mottled by the shadows of the wavelets. There was no sign of hippos just yet, but the river twisted this way and that, and there were many turns still to be negotiated. A herd of hippos might be behind any of these, waiting to demonstrate their well-known irascibility.

"I suppose it is better to be taken by a hippo than a crocodile," the boatman went on. "If a hippo bites you in two, then you do not have much time to think. It is very quick . . . particularly if he gets your head in that big mouth of his. Then it must be like night coming suddenly. Very dark, I think, Mma."

Mma Ramotswe tried to distract him. "There is a very interesting bird in the reeds over there, Rra. Did you see him?"

"That bird is very common, Mma," said the boatman. "You will see many of those birds in the Delta. You must not worry about them. They are harmless."

"I was not worried about the bird," said Mma Ramotswe. "I was just pointing it out."

"Of course," went on the boatman, "if a crocodile gets you, then that is very different. That is not a good way to go. You've heard about the roll?"

Mma Ramotswe said nothing. Mma Makutsi was staring ahead; she too was mute.

The boatman was warming to his subject, raising his voice to make sure that both his passengers heard. "The crocodile gets you in his jaws. Then he takes you down under the water and he rolls over and over, spinning you round and round. This is to make you drown. Then he drags you away to his lair, which is usually under roots at the edge of a riverbank, rather like that place over there. See it? That is a good place for a crocodile to have his lair."

Mma Makutsi did not dare so much as switch her gaze to the side; Mma Ramotswe glanced towards the bank, and then looked back ahead.

"Crocodiles don't like fresh meat," the boatman explained. "They much prefer to eat their prey when it's a bit rotten. That is why they put you in their lair, you see . . ."

"Excuse me, Rra," said Mma Ramotswe suddenly. "This is all very interesting, but I do not think that it is a good idea to tell people these things when they are on the water. There are some stories that are better told on the land."

"Yes," said Mma Makutsi. "That is true. We do not want you to speak, Rra. We are not in a mood for conversation."

The boatman looked puzzled. Women, he thought. It was always the same: men were interested in crocodiles and hippos and how they behaved; women were not. It was very difficult to understand. What did women think about? He had never worked out an answer to this, in spite of having had five wives. Perhaps I shall never understand them, he thought.

CHAPTER FIFTEEN

AT EAGLE ISLAND CAMP

THEY ARRIVED SAFELY. There were no hippos, and no crocodiles—or at least, none that they saw, and the two elephants they spotted, two young males standing under a canopy of large marula trees, were a safe distance away and completely uninterested in the passing boat.

Mma Ramotswe arranged for the boatman to return the following day. She and Mma Makutsi would spend the night in the camp, staying in the staff village with one of the women who worked in the kitchens. This woman was a friend of the cousin in Maun—again, a connection that could be deemed sufficiently close to allow for a request for hospitality. Of course, hospitality would be repaid at some time in the future: somebody from the camp would be in Gaborone, and would appear at the house in need of a bed for the night, or for several nights, and a meal, or several meals. Mma Ramotswe did not resent this, as it was the old Botswana morality in action: you helped people who had helped you, or who knew people whom you had helped.

The boatman disappeared down a winding branch of the river, whistling tunelessly. "That man is very tactless," said Mma

Makutsi. "He has no idea of when is the right time to talk about certain things. Imagine if we had been visitors, Mma. Imagine if we had been Swedish! We would have wanted to go straight back to Sweden, I think."

"He was only trying to be helpful," said Mma Ramotswe. "But you are right, Mma, he would not be the best tour guide in Botswana, I think. He would not be very reassuring for . . . for Swedish people."

Mma Makutsi had more to say on the subject. "I was not frightened, Mma. I was not worried."

"Of course not," said Mma Ramotswe.

"But the Swedes . . ."

"Yes, of course. The Swedes. You are right to be concerned, Mma." Mma Ramotswe, having straightened her dress, was looking towards the camp buildings a short distance away. A man in a khaki uniform was making his way towards them. He lifted an arm, waving, and greeted them politely as he came closer.

"You are Mma Ramotswe, are you, Mma?"

Mma Ramotswe inclined her head. "I am that lady," she said. "And this is Mma Makutsi."

"Assistant detective," said Mma Makutsi quickly.

The man announced himself as the deputy manager. He had heard from the camp's head office in Maun about Mma Ramotswe's telephone call a couple of days earlier, explaining her mission. They were pleased, he said, that one of their guests had been so impressed with her visit as to leave a gift to one of the guides. "We are very happy about that, Mma, and we would like to help you. If you tell us who this American lady was, then we can find out which guide looked after her."

They walked back towards the camp. The deputy manager would show them, he said, to the staff quarters, where they would be spending the night. Afterwards, they could come and have tea with the manager and the senior guide and talk about their mission. As they walked, Mma Ramotswe looked about her: she was still in her country, in Botswana, but it was a different Botswana from the one she knew. The vegetation here seemed very different—the trees were higher, the leaves greener. There were palm trees among the mopani and acacia; there were creepers and vines; everything was denser.

"This is a very beautiful place," said Mma Ramotswe.

"That is why people come here," said the deputy manager. "They come because they want to find a beautiful place. That is what people want."

"There are many beautiful places," said Mma Makutsi.

The deputy manager looked at her appreciatively, as if impressed by the wisdom of her observation. "I think that you are right," he said.

Nothing more was said on the rest of the walk to the staff quarters. The woman with whom they were staying met them there, and took them to her small thatched house—a couple of rooms, one of which she had cleared for her guests. Mma Ramotswe looked at the floor, on which two reed sleeping mats had been laid. Beside each mat, a glass jam jar filled with water had been placed, each holding a small bunch of white and yellow flowers. The floor had been recently swept, and bore the marks of the brush, tiny scratch-like lines. A rough cupboard, unsteady on its legs she imagined, stood against the rear wall, ready for the guests' possessions. The cupboard had been emptied of its contents and its door now stood ajar. This, she thought, is half a house, and it has been cleared for us.

"You should not have done this just for us," she said to the woman, who had introduced herself as Mma Sepoi.

Mma Sepoi smiled, and dropped a knee in a small curtsy. "You are my guests, Mma. I want you to be comfortable."

They settled in, Mma Sepoi telling them about her life while they placed in the rickety cupboard the few possessions they had brought with them. It was an ability that Mme Ramotswe always admired—that of encapsulating a whole life, and often the life of an entire family, in a few sentences. So many people, she had discovered, could do it, and effortlessly too; in her own case, she needed time. Where would one start? With Obed Ramotswe meeting her mother, bashful and hesitant about marriage, when he came back for a break from his work in the mines? With her return to Mochudi and that terrible stormy night when her mother, in circumstances that were yet to be fully explained, wandered onto the railway line that ran from Bulawayo down to Mafikeng? With those early days at the school high above Mochudi, where one might hear drifting from down below the sound of cattle bells?

"I have worked here for four years," said Mma Sepoi. "I am very happy. Some people, you know, that go into one job and then another, they say, *This job does not suit me; it has this, that, or the next thing wrong with it.* You know people like that, Mma Ramotswe? There are many of them. Not me. I came here after I had worked as a cleaning lady in Maun. Before that I had a job at Jack's Camp, with the old man, not the son, but the father before him. They are very good people. They know this country better than most people, Mma. And before that I was in Nata, from the time when I was a girl. My father was a policeman there. He was very good at catching stock thieves. If a cattle thief saw him coming, just walking along the road, he would run. Like that. Off. And my father would run after him and catch him because he had been in the police running team. He was a No. 1 police runner. And his father, my grandfather, was from Francistown, and his cattle were all drowned in a big flood on the Shashi River. That happened a long time ago, Mma."

"A lot has happened in your life," said Mma Makutsi. "You have had a very eventful life."

Mma Sepoi acknowledged the compliment. "I have had many things that have happened to me. But I am not complaining. I say that everything that happens has a lesson in it. You look at it and you say, 'That happened because of this thing.' And then when it happens next, you know why it happened in the first place." She paused to take a breath. "That is the way I look at things, Mma."

Mma Makutsi took off her glasses and polished them. "Are there many animals here, Mma?" she asked. The question was casually posed, but Mma Ramotswe detected an edge to it.

"Oh, there are many," said Mma Sepoi. She pointed out of the door behind her. "Keep this door closed at night, Mma."

Mma Makutsi redoubled her polishing efforts. "I always keep my door closed at night," she said nervously. "It is safer that way."

"Especially here," said Mma Sepoi. "I got up the other night because I heard something sniffing at my door. I have a saucepan by my bed and I bang it against the wall to make a noise. Lions don't like saucepans, Mma."

Mma Makutsi swallowed. "I have heard that."

"I'll leave one by your bed, Mma. So if you need it, you can make a noise." Mma Sepoi paused. "Of course it may not have been a lion," she said.

Mma Makutsi looked relieved. A warthog would not frighten anybody; nor an anteater. "Of course. It may have been something else."

"A leopard, perhaps," said Mma Sepoi. "They are very dangerous too, you know."

Later, on their way over to the office in the main camp, Mma Ramotswe noticed that her assistant was walking very close to her, almost bumping into her as they made their way along the narrow path. She tried not to smile; it had never occurred to her that Mma Makutsi would be nervous about being in the Delta. Had Mma Makutsi had a bad experience up in Bobonong, when she was a girl? Sometimes people could be afraid of snakes, for instance, if they had encountered a snake as a child. She had known somebody who had a tendency to faint at the very mention of snakes; and another, she now remembered, who panicked at the sight of a spider. Mma Ramotswe, of course, had a healthy respect for wild animals, but understood that they were generally quite harmless unless one intruded upon their territory, which she had no intention of doing. Mind you, she told herself, the river, on which she and Mma Makutsi had travelled earlier that day, was the territory of the hippopotamus, and the crocodile, and . . .

They arrived at the camp office. The manager appeared—a tall man, a South African, who stooped to shake hands with them. "I have heard why you have come here, Mma Ramotswe," he said. "Our chief guide is here. He is called Mighty, and he keeps the roster of who looks after each guest. He will tell you who this fortunate man is."

They went from the office to the area beside the water where, under the spreading boughs of a tree, chairs had been arranged around an open fireplace. The water was clogged with reeds, over which a brightly coloured bird hovered in flight. A guide, wearing the ubiquitous khaki uniform of the Delta, was standing beside one of the chairs, staring at the place where the fire had been laid, poking at the cold ashes with a stick. He looked up when they approached.

"This is Mighty," said the manager.

Mighty shook hands with the visitors. Mma Ramotswe found herself warming to him immediately, recognising in him the real countryman, the type that her father had been. Obed Ramotswe had known all there was to know about cattle; she felt that this man knew everything there was to know about the animals of the wild, which was the same sort of thing.

"Do you remember an American lady called Mrs. Grant?" asked Mma Ramotswe.

Mighty looked doubtful. "We get many Americans, Mma. Germans, Swedes, British—all of these people. It is difficult to remember one person out of many hundreds. How many years ago was it, Mma?"

"Four. It was in June or July of that year, Rra."

"Oh," said Mighty. "That is a long time ago, Mma. A long time."

"She stayed for almost a week, Rra. She was very happy here."

Mighty looked out over the water. "A week? That is unusual. Most of our visitors are here for two or three days. An American lady? Now, I think I can remember a lady who stayed. Yes, she was a very pleasant lady. She was very happy here, you are right." He paused. "We have the old duty rosters in the office. The details will be there. Should I get the page for that week?"

The manager and Mma Ramotswe both agreed that this was the thing to do. Mighty went off, and while he was gone Mma Ramotswe looked around the camp—at the tempting chairs and the tables beyond, set out for lunch. It would be good to be a guest here, she thought; one might sit in one of these chairs and drink something cold—lemonade, perhaps—and then progress to the lunch table and eat . . . She brought herself back to reality. She and Mma Makutsi were not here to sit about—as if they were members of some double comfort safari club—they were here to find somebody, to talk to him, and then to return to Gaborone.

When Mighty returned he took a crumpled document out of his pocket. "I have looked in the roster for June, Mma, and I found it straightaway," he said, handing the paper to Mma Ramotswe. "I have taken it from the book. This is it."

Mma Ramotswe looked down at the piece of paper. It was not complicated, and she saw immediately the information that she needed. Against the name of each guide was written the name of a guest, or group of guests, together with the days during which the guide would be on duty. Mrs. Grant, she saw, had been looked after by a guide called Tebogo. It was a common enough name. "So it was this Tebogo," she said, holding up the paper. "He was the one who looked after the American lady."

Mighty nodded. "He was the one."

Mma Makutsi looked over her shoulder. "So that's it, Mma. We have found out what we came for. Maybe we should go back to Maun now."

Mma Ramotswe turned to her assistant. "But we cannot go back, Mma. We have just arrived. The boatman won't be back until tomorrow. You heard him."

Mma Makutsi looked disappointed, but seeing Mighty looking at her, she made an effort to mask her concern.

"Don't be afraid, Mma," said Mighty suddenly. "Everything is very safe here."

Mma Makutsi gave a nonchalant laugh. "Scared, Rra?" she said. "Who is scared?"

You are, thought Mma Ramotswe, but said nothing.

"Tebogo will be back soon," said Mighty, glancing at the sinking sun. "He has taken some people on a game walk. He will not be long."

Mma Ramotswe noticed the glance at the sun. People who lived in towns had stopped doing that—they had watches to enslave them. Here in the bush it was different: what the watch said was less important than what the sun said, and that, she thought, was the way it should be.

SHE DID NOT NOTICE Tebogo arriving; suddenly he was there, having joined their company while her attention was diverted by a playful monkey that was taunting them from the safety of the tree.

"This is Tebogo," said Mighty.

Mma Ramotswe turned round to see a tall man in khaki uniform standing at the edge of the circle of chairs. He was in his late forties, she thought, possibly slightly younger, but certainly a man with some experience of life. He had an open countenance, with the same clear look in his eyes that she had seen in Mighty's. It was something to do with being a game-spotter, she imagined; these people were used to gazing out into the distance, picking up the tiniest clue of an animal's presence—a change in the colour of background vegetation, an unusual movement of leaves, a shape that was wrong for its place. Looking for such things perhaps explained this quality in their eyes—the brightness, the quick movements.

Mighty continued with his explanation. He told Tebogo that Mma Ramotswe had come to see him "all the way from Gaborone," and that she had "important news." At this, a shadow passed over Tebogo's face, a look of alarm, and she said quickly, "Good news, Rra."

He looked at her expectantly, and then glanced again at Mighty, as if for confirmation.

She went straight to the point. "There was a lady you looked after, Rra. She was called Mrs. Grant."

For a moment he looked confused, but then he nodded. "Yes, maybe, Mma. Maybe."

"She was here for some days," went on Mma Ramotswe.

Tebogo nodded. "I am not sure, Mma. It is not easy to remember one person after a long time. It is difficult, Mma."

"It must be," said Mma Ramotswe. "But I think that you people have good memories. It is your job that helps you to remember. You see things and you remember them."

Mighty laughed. "Sometimes, Mma, sometimes. Not always."

"Well, Mma Grant remembered you," said Mma Ramotswe. "You were very kind to her."

Tebogo looked down modestly. "It is our job, Mma. We are kind to people because it is our job. Not just me—everybody here."

For a few moments, Mma Ramotswe was silent as she weighed his remark. No, it was not true. They were professional in their dealings with their guests, and that meant they were courteous and attentive, but kindness was another matter—it required that there be something in the heart. She looked at Mighty; he had it too, she suspected—that quality of kindness that visitors to the country so often remarked upon.

"I think that you were kind to her, Rra," she said quietly. "But I have not come to talk about that. I have come to tell you what has happened to that lady. She is late, I'm afraid to say."

She watched. Again, she was sure that she was right: he was upset.

"I am very sorry to hear that, Mma. I'm sure that she was a nice lady."

She knew that he meant it. If there was anything that she had learned in her years as a private detective, it was the ability to tell when somebody meant what they said.

"I believe she was, Rra," she said. "And a generous one too."

Mma Makutsi had been quiet until now, but this was her opportunity. "Generous to you," she said.

Tebogo looked inquiringly at Mma Makutsi. "Oh?"

"Yes," said Mma Ramotswe. "She spoke to her lawyer before she died. Over in America. She spoke to him, and told him that she wanted to give you some money. And now that is why we are here. We have come to find you and tell you about this money."

For a moment Tebogo simply stared at her. Then he shook his head. "I cannot believe this, Mma. It cannot be true."

"It is," said Mma Ramotswe. "Mma Grant has left you three thousand dollars. That is . . ."

"Almost twenty thousand pula," interjected Mighty.

Tebogo shook his head again. Then he smiled. "That is . . . It is . . ."

"It is very good luck," said Mighty.

"I am very grateful," said Tebogo. He let out a low whistle. "Twenty thousand pula!"

"Be careful that you do not spend it all at once," said Mma Makutsi.

Mma Ramotswe looked at her assistant. She had a tendency to bossiness, she thought, and she should have a word with her about it at some point. But it was difficult to broach the subject of a person's failings, particularly if that person was Mma Makutsi, with her ever so slightly prickly nature. Perhaps her shoes would say something; Mma Makutsi had once, jokingly— and she *must* have been joking—told her that her shoes occasion- ally gave her advice. Well, perhaps they could tell her not to be so bossy. They must have witnessed it, after all—shoes see every- thing; there are no secrets we can keep from our shoes.

"I'm sure that Tebogo will be very careful," said Mma Ramotswe, adding, "and I really don't think we need to tell him how to look after his money."

"I will put it in the bank," said Tebogo. "And then I will spend it later."

"That sounds very wise," said Mma Ramotswe.

"There are school fees for my son," he went on.

Mma Ramotswe nodded her approval. "Yes, that would be a good thing to spend it on."

"And my mother is very old," Tebogo continued.

"Then you can make her comfortable," said Mma Ramotswe.

"And I can buy some cattle for my cattle post."

Mma Ramotswe thought that a good idea too. "That too. School fees, mother, and cattle. All of these are very fine purposes, Rra."

Tebogo looked thoughtful. "I have just remembered something," he said. "I have a letter from a lady in America. I still have it. It may be that lady, that Mma Grant."

Mighty explained that this was quite common. "People often write to us," he said. "They write to thank us, or they send us a postcard to show where else they have been."

"I keep all these things," said Tebogo. "Would you like to see it? I can go and fetch it from my place. I think I know where it will be."

Mma Ramotswe said that she would, and Tebogo walked off to the staff quarters to fetch the letter. A few minutes later he returned, clutching a large envelope. From this he drew out a typed letter to which was attached a couple of newspaper cuttings and a photograph.

"This is what she sent me," he explained. "Those pages from the newspaper are about a man from her home town who was breeding ostriches. I had showed her some ostriches, and she thought I might be interested in that. And there is a photograph of me and her standing together outside the camp. I remember this lady. I had just forgotten that she was called Mma Grant."

He was clearly exhilarated by the news that Mma Ramotswe had given him, and he spoke quickly, the excitement showing in his voice. Mma Ramotswe took the sheaf of papers from him, and looked at the press cuttings. She found it touching that a woman like Mrs. Grant, who lived so far from the world of this man, should have sent him things to read from her newspaper. But that was how people were: they reached out to one another, no matter what dividing chasms lay between them—chasms of geography, and nation, and language; in spite of all these, people could still look at others and see that we were all the same, at least in those things that mattered, those things of the spirit, of the heart— human things.

"Ostriches," she muttered.

"Yes," said Tebogo. "I have read the articles. It is very interesting. But I felt a bit sorry, Mma."

Mma Ramotswe looked up sharply. "Sorry for Mma Grant?"

He shook his head. "No, for the ostriches. They are so far away from Africa. They are living in a cold place. They must be very sad."

"They do not know about any of that," said Mma Makutsi firmly. "An ostrich that is born in another place does not know about Africa. And they do not have very big heads, Rra. So they do not know where they are."

Tebogo gave Mma Makutsi a challenging look. "Animals and birds know exactly where they are," he said reproachfully. "They know many things, Mma."

Mma Ramotswe folded up the ostrich articles and detached the photograph from the letter. "So this is . . ." She stopped. She had seen a photograph of Mrs. Grant in the obituary that the lawyer had sent her. The late Mrs. Grant was thin, even gaunt. This Mrs. Grant was by contrast traditionally built. The late Mrs. Grant had grey hair, cut short, and a prominent nose. This Mrs. Grant had blonde, shoulder-length hair and a very small nose. They were not the same person; she had absolutely no doubt about it.

CHAPTER SIXTEEN

MOST UNFORTUNATE

IT WAS FORTUNATE that Mma Makutsi chose this moment of dismaying discovery to engage Tebogo in conversation about the antics of the monkey in the tree above them. The monkey, which had been joined by three or four of its troop, was chattering excitedly, competing with its fellows over some morsel it had found in the higher branches. Leaving her assistant, Mma Ramotswe took Mighty to one side.

"There is something wrong," she whispered.

Mighty drew in his breath. "You don't think he deserves the money?"

"No. It's not that. It's the wrong person."

Mighty looked puzzled. Glancing over his shoulder to check that they could not be overheard by Tebogo, he assured her that there was no question but that Tebogo had looked after Mrs. Grant. "It is in the book," he said. "And he remembers her." He gestured to the letter. "That letter is signed by Mrs. Grant, isn't it? Yes, look at it. That says *Grant.*"

Mma Ramotswe frowned. "I know," she whispered. "I know that. But that lady in the picture is not Mrs. Grant. I have her photograph with my things in the room. I'll show you, if you like. That is not the lady."

Mighty made a gesture of helplessness. "I don't see how this can be," he said.

Mma Ramotswe fiddled anxiously with the papers. "I don't know what to do," she said. "I cannot pay the money to the wrong man. I have my duty to Mrs. Grant's lawyer, a certain Mr. Maxwell. He is my client, Rra. Can you see that?"

Mighty nodded, again looking furtively at Tebogo. "I understand, Mma. But I just don't see how this can be. A lady called Mrs. Grant came to this camp . . ."

Mma Ramotswe took hold of his forearm. "Hold on, Rra. You said that a lady called Mrs. Grant came to the camp . . ."

"I did. And I have already shown you the evidence of that."

Mma Ramotswe drew him further away from the other two, who were still engaged in their observation of the monkeys. "A lady called Mrs. Grant," said Mma Ramotswe. She spoke slowly and deliberately, as if testing each word. "Do you think that Grant is a common name, Rra? I've certainly seen it before. Have you?"

Mighty considered this. "I think so," he said. "We've had other Grants before. Maybe it's a common name in America, like . . . like Tebogo in Botswana. Or Ramotswe . . ."

Mma Ramotswe smiled, but did not let the joke distract her. "You've had other Grants before, you say. But not at the same time."

"No, not at the same time."

It was all falling into place. "Mighty," she said, "what if there were two Mma Ramotswes? Or two Mma Grants?"

Mighty frowned. "Two Mma Ramotswes?" He stared at her, and then he put his hand to his cheek and stroked it. "Oh," he said. Then, "Oh," again.

"Oh," echoed Mma Ramotswe. She looked in his eyes. He was a sharp-witted man. He understood. But there was one final piece of the jigsaw to fit into place. "Can you think of another camp with an animal in its name?"

Mighty answered quickly. "Our neighbour," he said. "Three miles away. Lion's Tail Camp."

"Can you take me there?" asked Mma Ramotswe.

Mighty looked doubtful. "Right now?"

"Yes. Right now, Rra."

"It's getting late. We'll have to go by boat."

"I'm ready to go."

Mighty still looked worried. "I don't like to travel on the water at night. It would be dark by the time we came back."

"Give me a torch," said Mma Ramotswe. "I shall sit in the front and shine it ahead of us. If there are any hippos, we shall see their eyes in the beam of the torch."

"You are a brave lady, Mma. Maybe that is why you're a detective."

Mma Ramotswe laughed. "I am no braver than anybody else." Was that true? she wondered. There was Mma Makutsi, after all . . . "I think that I shall leave my assistant back here. I don't think that she will want to come."

WITH MIGHTY'S EXPERT NAVIGATION through the spreading channels of the Delta, it took them barely half an hour to reach Lion's Tail Camp. It was a more modest camp than Eagle Island, with smaller, tented rooms for the visitors, but still with that stylish old-safari feel that Botswana did so well. The manager was away in Maun, but the head guide, Moripe Moripe, an old friend of Mighty, greeted them warmly and listened attentively to Mma

Ramotswe's story. As her explanation drew to a close, he started to nod encouragingly.

"Yes, Mma," he said. "I remember that lady. Mma Grant was here at the time. You are right." He paused, as if fetching something from the dim recesses of memory. "It was July, Mma. I remember it because that was the month that my grandmother became late."

"Are you sure of that? July?"

He nodded. "Yes, I am."

She felt the familiar excitement that came with the solving of a mystery. But in this case, although she was pleased to have found out what happened, she felt appalled at what she had done. She had raised the hopes of a man who would now have to be told that the fortune he thought he was going to receive would no longer be his.

She reached into the bag she had brought with her and took out the obituary cutting. "Is this that lady?" she asked.

Moripe Moripe examined the photograph. "That is the lady. She had hair like that. That is her."

"Are you sure?" asked Mma Ramotswe, looking into his eyes. It seemed unlikely to her that somebody would remember one guest of many, and after a few years had passed.

Moripe Moripe met her gaze. "I am very sure, Mma. If you spend a long time with somebody, and you talk to them a lot, then you remember them."

Mma Ramotswe skirted round what she thought was a general observation. "Who was the guide who looked after her, Rra?"

Moripe Moripe looked surprised by the question. "But I've just told you, Mma. It was me. I was the one. I looked after her for five or six days. That is why I remember her."

It was then that Mighty intervened. "You can trust this man,

Mma Ramotswe," he said. "He is well known to us. I know him. And Tebogo knows him too."

The mention of the name Tebogo appeared to amuse Moripe Moripe. "That is a good man," he said.

"Moripe Moripe is going to marry Tebogo's sister," said Mighty. "They are good friends."

They are good friends. It took a moment or two for the words to sink in, as is often the case when something is said that suddenly offers a way out of an impossible situation. *They are good friends.* As she repeated the words to herself, Mma Ramotswe felt an immense relief. *Bride price,* she thought. *Lobola.* It was often there in Botswana, in the background, playing an important role in people's affairs, like a strong wind that always blew, or a strong current under the surface of water. Always there.

They had not yet told Moripe Moripe about the legacy, but now she felt she could. "I have a curious story to tell you, Rra," she said. "But first, I think you should sit down."

They sat down more or less where they were, under a tree, with the sun burning down over the swamps in a flourish of red. "This story is one of extraordinary coincidence, Rra," Mma Ramotswe began. And she told him of the two Mrs. Grants arriving one shortly after the other, and of their going to nearby camps. It seemed unlikely, but one could see how it had happened. Unlikely things do happen, said Mma Ramotswe, and she knew, for she had seen many such things happen in her job, and had long since come to the conclusion that the extraordinary was often not quite as extraordinary as people imagined it to be. Then, after relating what had happened, she went on to tell him of the deathbed request by Mrs. Grant—the real Mrs. Grant. "And that is what I have come to tell you, Rra. You have been given twenty thousand pula. It is her way of saying thank you."

Moripe Moripe took the news calmly. "That is very kind, Mma. Very kind."

Mma Ramotswe glanced at Mighty, who looked down at the ground in silent sympathy. How was she going to tell him that she had already promised the money to another, even if it was his future brother-in-law?

"Tell me, Rra," began Mma Ramotswe. "You are going to marry Tebogo's sister. Are the parents late—her parents?"

"They are. They are both sadly late."

"So *lobola* will be payable to the uncles . . ." She hardly dared hope. But you had to hope; you had to. Not only about this, but about everything.

"To the brother. There is only one uncle and he is . . ." Moripe Moripe tapped the side of his head. "He is very happy, but he does not know what is going on. He thinks every day is Sunday. It is very strange."

Mma Ramotswe thought it would be improper to let out a cry of delight. It could be misinterpreted, she felt, and she would not want Moripe Moripe to think that she took pleasure in the plight of his future uncle-in-law.

"So you have to pay the *lobola* for your future wife to Tebogo?"

Moripe Moripe looked glum, but almost immediately brightened. "Yes, and I was going to find it very difficult, Mma. I have asked him whether we can defer the payment. My sister has been ill and has many children. I have had to support them."

"So you have been able to pay nothing?"

"Yes. But now . . . Well, now I can give him the money."

"He thinks he already has it," said Mma Ramotswe. "And in a way, he has."

She shivered. The sun had disappeared now, and the air had

become cooler. It was a very good end to the day, she thought. A debt had disappeared. A mistake had been made, and been rectified by an extraordinary coincidence. No, she thought, nothing is extraordinary. Such things have happened before, and will happen again. There were probably numerous Mrs. Grants, travelling the world and causing confusion. It was nothing unusual.

THE TRIP BACK by boat was uneventful. Mma Ramotswe sat in the bow, sweeping the river ahead of them with the beam of Mighty's powerful yellow torch. On one or two occasions she thought that she saw eyes shining back at her, but it was only a trick of the water, a stone on the bank, a leaf on the surface, and there was no sign of any hippo. When they reached the camp, Mighty took her to the kitchen, where she was given a plate of food. Mma Makutsi had already eaten, she was told, and had gone back to their room with a paraffin lamp. Mighty stayed with her while she ate, and then conducted her back to the staff quarters, his torch again sweeping the darkness for animal hazards. "We have an old elephant who comes into the camp," he said. "He is not aggressive, but we wouldn't like to bump into him at night." She agreed. She would not like to bump into anything at night, unless it was a meerkat, perhaps, or a dassie. Even then . . .

Mma Makutsi had settled on her sleeping mat, the paraffin lamp still burning in a corner of the room. Mma Ramotswe told her of the meeting with Moripe Moripe and of the unexpected, but welcome, outcome. "We made a bad mistake," she said. "I was dreading telling Tebogo that it was not him after all who would get the money. Now I can tell him the truth. I can tell him about the mistake, but reassure him that he will be getting most of it, if not all, as the *lobola* that Moripe Moripe owes him. So everybody should be happy enough."

"That is an excellent outcome," said Mma Makutsi. "There are very few cases when you can say at the end that everybody is happy."

"And we are happy too," said Mma Ramotswe. "This has been a successful business trip, and a very comfortable safari that we have had."

"I am not sure that I like safaris," said Mma Makutsi. "Maybe I'm a town girl at heart."

Mma Ramotswe said nothing to this. It was getting late, and she was tired. So she went to the lamp and turned down the wick until there was just a tiny flickering of the flame, and then no light at all. She lay in the darkness, mulling over what had happened that day. Mma Makutsi muttered something that she did not quite catch, but was probably *Goodnight*. She said *Goodnight*, softly, in case Mma Makutsi was already asleep, or drifting off.

Later that night, much later, Mma Ramotswe awoke. At first she had no idea why—perhaps it was a bad dream—but she suddenly found herself wide awake. The curtain across the window made the room pitch dark, and it was silent too, with only the faint sound of Mma Makutsi's breathing on the other side. Then she heard the sound. It must have penetrated the veils of sleep and prodded her into consciousness. There it was—a curious sniffing sound.

Her thoughts went immediately to snakes. There was a particular sort of snake, the puff adder, that made a sound like that when it was agitated. Those snakes were always finding their way inside and causing terrible trouble. Perhaps there was one in the room already, sliding its way across the floor to where she lay. She sat bolt upright. The sound came again, and this time she was able to locate it as being outside the room. It was definitely outside, and she had decided now that this was no snake.

She rose to her feet and crept silently across the room to the low window. Very slowly, she drew the curtain and peered outside. The moon was a sliver away from fullness, bathing the staff quarters and the surrounding bush in silver light. Her eyes took a moment to adjust, and then everything was clear, sharply delineated enough to throw ghostly moon shadows on the ground.

She looked, and saw, barely an arm's length away from the gauze window, looking directly in at her, a fully grown lion. He looked straight at her, surprised, and she saw for a moment the moon in his eyes. Then, with a sudden tensing of muscle and a whipping movement of his tail, he turned and shot back into the bush. It happened so quickly that she wondered for a moment whether she had imagined it, but there was a rustle of leaves in the bush where he had run, and that was proof that this was no dream, no illusion.

She heard her heart thumping within her, her mouth dry from shock and fear. She stared at the place where only seconds ago the lion had been; she would not have been surprised had she seen his shadow in the moonlight, imprinted on the ground, as a shadow will register on a photographic plate, caught, as now, in silver.

She let the curtain fall back into place. She made her way back to her sleeping mat. She would not wake Mma Makutsi, nor, she thought, would she tell her about this the following morning. There were some things it was better that people—and Mma Makutsi in particular—did not know.

THEY STARTED their journey home the next day. The boatman did not engage them in unsettling conversation, but kept up his tuneless whistle for much of the way back. Then, picking up the van from the cousin's house, they started the long drive home.

They talked about all sorts of things on the way back: about weddings and children and money. About cattle. About jealousy and envy and love. About cakes. About friends and enemies and people they remembered who had gone away, or changed, or even died. About everything, really.

They stayed overnight in Francistown, as they had started late from Maun and needed the break. Their hotel was cheap and noisy, and there were mosquitoes to keep them from sleeping. In the morning they left without breakfasting, eager to get away from the smell of the place, and stopped at a small village on the main road, where they bought doughnuts and large mugs of tea. By noon they were back in Gaborone.

Mma Ramotswe dropped Mma Makutsi off at her house and made her way to the office to attend to the mail, which Charlie would have picked up from the postbox for them. She was going through the small number of letters she had received when Mma Mateleke arrived.

"I do not have an appointment, Mma," her visitor said. "But you do not need an appointment to see an old friend, do you?"

Mma Ramotswe felt tired. She was not in the mood to see anybody, but she could not turn Mma Mateleke away. "I am always happy to see you," she said.

"Good," said Mma Mateleke. "Since I saw you last, my husband has been very attentive. He has tried to take me out to dinner, to the Portuguese restaurant—you know the one? But I do not have time for such things, Mma, particularly when the invitation is the result of guilt over an affair. Men are very easy to read, aren't they?"

Mma Ramotswe did not reply, and so Mma Mateleke continued. "So tell me, Mma, have you found out that my husband is having an affair? Who is the woman?"

Mma Ramotswe sighed. She wanted to be at home; she did

not want to have to give Mma Mateleke the advice that she had planned to give her. She just did not have the energy. But she could hardly refuse to answer, and so she said, "I have looked into it, Mma. And I am satisfied of one thing: your husband is not having an affair. No girlfriend. Nothing."

Mma Mateleke stared at her. "You are sure, Mma?" the midwife asked. "You are sure that he is not seeing somebody?"

Mma Ramotswe suddenly became very alert, very aware of what was happening. And at that moment, simply by looking at her friend, she knew. *Mma Mateleke was disappointed. She wanted to hear that the Reverend Mateleke was having an affair.* That realisation made it all clear. A wife would not be disappointed to hear that her husband was not having an affair, *unless she herself was having an affair.* If she was having an affair, it would be much easier for her to blame him for the breakdown of the marriage if he were having one too. It was very simple.

Mma Ramotswe stared at her friend. "I can tell that you are disappointed, Mma. It shows."

Mma Mateleke made a dismissive gesture, but said nothing.

Mma Ramotswe thought of what Mr. J.L.B. Matekoni had said to her about the man he had met on the Lobatse Road, the man who appeared to have driven out to rescue Mma Mateleke when her car broke down. He had wondered whether that man was Mma Mateleke's lover, but Mma Ramotswe had rather dismissed the suggestion. He had mentioned the man's name, though, and it came back to her now. "So tell me, Mma," she said. "How long have you been having an affair with that man—with Mr. Ntirang?"

Mma Mateleke's eyes narrowed. "Ntirang?" And her voice, small and strained, provided further confirmation.

"I cannot help you in this matter," said Mma Ramotswe wearily. "All I can say is this: I believe that your husband is very fond of you. I believe that he is anxious because I suspect that he knows. So you must now decide what to do. I cannot make that decision for you. You must choose."

Mma Mateleke said nothing. She stood up, hesitated for a moment, and then left the room without saying goodbye. Mma Ramotswe sat down and closed her eyes. The long drive had tired her to the extent of being incapable of making tea. But Mr. Polopetsi came in, saw the state she was in, and made tea for her. He did not ask her why she looked so despondent, so defeated, but sat there, silently, sharing her tea, until she was ready to gather herself and go home.

CHAPTER SEVENTEEN

A DAM OF HEALING WATERS

THREE DAYS LATER, with everything back to normal after the Maun trip, they were sitting in the office when Mma Ramotswe noticed that it was time, as it so often seemed to be, for morning tea. Mma Makutsi put on the kettle, her accustomed task, and lined up the two teapots at the ready.

"Be sure to use the big one for the ordinary tea," said Mma Ramotswe from the other side of the room. "That would be best."

Mma Makutsi hesitated. "But it is the one you have always used," she ventured. "I do not want to change things . . ."

Mma Ramotswe was insistent. "No, Mma. We have already discussed this. I am happy with that small teapot for my red bush tea. I am happy to change."

The words *I am happy to change* made Mma Makutsi think. What Mma Ramotswe said about herself was probably true: when change came along, she often seemed to welcome it, or at least accept it. There were many people who did not—who harped on about the past and how things used to be, who never understood that some things have to be different as time passes. Mma Ramotswe was not one of these . . . Mma Makutsi stopped.

No, perhaps she was. She always said that the old Botswana morality should not be changed; she always went for mid-morning tea at the President Hotel on Saturdays and did not want that changed; and she had been very reluctant indeed to change her van. And yet, there were many novel things that Mma Ramotswe seemed to accept. Perhaps she was a mixture, as most of us were; we accepted some changes—changes we liked—and resisted others—changes we did not like. Yes, that must be it.

She made the tea as her employer instructed. That was a good thing, as that morning not only did Mr. Polopetsi come in with his mug ready for filling, but also Charlie and Fanwell, and, last of all, Mr. J.L.B. Matekoni. He did not linger, but poured himself a large cup and then returned to the garage, where there was a tricky repair being made to an important car. And as well as the entire staff, there was a visitor who wanted tea that morning: Mma Potokwane. She arrived just as Charlie and Fanwell were draining the last drops from their mugs, and caused their rapid departure. Even Charlie, who held few people in awe, was wary of Mma Potokwane, who seemed to remind him of all that was most powerful and daunting in Botswana womanhood.

It was not that Mma Potokwane had ever *said* very much to Charlie. It was true that she had once asked him what his long-term plans were, and asked the question in such a way as to imply that she at least could tell at a glance that he had none. It was true that she had once said to Mma Ramotswe—in his hearing—that he reminded her of a young man at the orphan farm who had turned out very badly and was now living in a cardboard box outside Lobatse. These comments were hardly confidence-building, and Charlie resented them. Yet it was not so much what she said that he objected to—it was the look that Mma Potokwane gave him. Normally Charlie could face down any look from a woman; after all, he had received many such looks from former girlfriends—looks of pure, distilled *reproach*—and knew how to deal with them. One simply looked the other way. But with Mma Potokwane it was different; her look, as Fanwell had once suggested, could stop the Mafikeng train in its tracks, and probably had.

If Mma Potokwane had a difficult relationship with Charlie, the same could be said of her dealings with Mma Makutsi. Mma Ramotswe was aware of this, and had attempted to reassure her assistant that the matron surely had no real objection to her; it was just the way that she looked, a question of manner, really. "It is difficult running an orphan farm," she said. "All those children. All those house mothers, all wanting this, that, and the next thing. And you know that Mma Potokwane would do anything for her people—anything."

That was certainly true. Mma Potokwane would stop at nothing to secure some benefit for the children in her care. She would cajole and wheedle until people gave the children what they needed, and when it came to dealings with officialdom, she would give no quarter. She always won, and the children benefited.

That morning when Mma Potokwane called out a cheerful *Ko! Ko!* and came into the room, Mma Makutsi exchanged a concerned glance with Mma Ramotswe, quickly thinking of reasons why she might have to leave the office on unspecified, but urgent, business. Her concern, though, was misplaced: it soon became apparent that Mma Potokwane had come on an errand of sympathy, and that sympathy was directed at Mma Makutsi herself.

"Mma Makutsi," she began, "I have heard of Mr. Radiphuti's accident. I am very sorry, Mma. And I am so sad for you, Mma, so sad."

Mma Makutsi looked up. Only two people so far had said

anything like this to her—Mma Ramotswe herself and the woman she had met on the bench outside the hospital. But here was a third.

"That is very kind of you, Mma. Thank you."

"I am always telling the drivers who deliver things to our place to watch out when they reverse. They do not listen, do they?"

Mma Makutsi nodded. "I think that is probably true. They are busy. They forget."

"Yes," said Mma Potokwane. "They probably think: *This is just another woman talking to me.* And now your poor Phuti has had this terrible injury. I am so sorry, Mma."

"Thank you, Mma."

Mma Potokwane sat down. "He is a lucky man to have you, Mma. When he comes out of hospital you can nurse him back to health. He will soon be up and about."

Mma Ramotswe now got up from her desk to pour tea for their visitor. "Actually, he is already out, Mma. He has made very good progress."

Mma Potokwane clapped her hands together. "That is very good news! So you are already looking after him. Give him plenty of meat, Mma. Breakfast, lunch, supper—good Botswana beef. That will make him strong. And vegetables. Also at breakfast, lunch and supper. Vegetables. Vitamin C." She paused. "You've got somebody at your house to help you?"

It was Mma Ramotswe who answered. She looked round and saw Mma Makutsi staring down at her hands, clasped together on the desk. "Well, Mma, it is rather difficult. You see, Mma Makutsi would like to look after Phuti, but he has an aunt, and this aunt has somehow managed to—"

Mma Potokwane stopped her. "Oh, I have met that woman. I cannot remember her name, but she has a . . ."

"Big head," Mma Makutsi supplied. "A big head, a bit like a melon." She sketched the dimensions of the head with her hands.

"Yes, that is her," said Mma Potokwane. "She is a very difficult woman. She was very rude to one of the house mothers once, at church, I think. She said that she was not putting enough money in the collection basket. I heard about that. The house mother had been crying. She said, *Some woman with a very big head made me very embarrassed.* I remember it."

Mma Ramotswe smiled, picturing the scene. The people who volunteered to take the collection at church were often of a rather stern type, she thought. "That is the woman who is now looking after Phuti," she said. "And she is trying to stop Mma Makutsi from seeing him."

Mma Potokwane put down her teacup with a clatter. "What? What is this?"

"She turns me away when I go to the house," explained Mma Makutsi. "She won't let me see Phuti, my own fiancé."

Mma Potokwane made a strange sound—a sort of eruption that came from deep within her, a small sound, perhaps, at its origin somewhere within her chest, but magnified tenfold as it came up through her matronly air passages, to emerge from her lips as an unmistakably disapproving snort. It was very like the sound, thought Mma Ramotswe, not without admiration, that a she-elephant makes when warning an intruder off her young.

"That is a piece of nonsense," said Mma Potokwane. "The place for a man who is recovering from an injury is with the lady who is almost married to him. That has always been so, and the world has not changed so much that it is any different now." She looked at Mma Ramotswe, as one matron to another. "Do you not agree with me, Mma Ramotswe?"

Mma Ramotswe inclined her head to signify that she did not

dissent. She agreed with Mma Potokwane on many things, but not all. Yet this was one area in which the agreement was perfect. Of course, this redoubtable woman, this defender of the interests of orphans—and fiancées—was right.

Mma Potokwane now looked out of the window, momentarily lost in thought. After a while she turned round and addressed Mma Makutsi. "Of course, it might be difficult for you to look after him all the time. You have your job, don't you?"

Mma Makutsi sighed. "It would be hard, Mma, but I would like to try."

"You live by yourself, don't you, Mma?" Mma Potokwane asked.

"Yes, I do. But I always get back by five-thirty. So he would only be by himself from . . ."

"From seven in the morning until five-thirty in the evening," said Mma Potokwane briskly. "That would not be very good for him, Mma. No, we must think of something else, and I believe that I have a solution."

Mma Ramotswe and Mma Makutsi exchanged glances.

"Yes," said Mma Potokwane. "I have been thinking. There is a room behind my office at the orphan farm. It is a very comfortable room that we sometimes use when we have visitors. Mr. Radiphuti could stay there, and that means there would be many people to look after him during the day. We have a nurse, as you know, and there is a house mother nearby who is a very good cook. Then you could come every evening, Mma Makutsi, and you could stay in my place. We have two extra bedrooms in our house. So you could see him in the evenings and all weekends. He would be very well looked after, I think."

For a moment or two Mma Makutsi did not move, but sat quite still, quite upright, as if transfixed. Then she removed her large glasses and polished them on the sleeve of her blouse. She put the glasses back on. "Oh, Mma . . . ," she began. She faltered. She had not received many kindnesses in her life, apart from those that she had had from Mma Ramotswe, and from Phuti, of course, and she was clearly finding it difficult to express what she felt. Mma Ramotswe could tell that, and she answered on her assistant's behalf. "That would be wonderful, Mma," she said. "I'm sure that Mma Makutsi would love that."

There was a vigorous nodding from Mma Makutsi.

"But then," Mma Ramotswe went on, "how do we get Phuti to hear about this? That aunt of his has cut off all communication. She is like a dog at the door."

Mma Potokwane let out another snort. "I will go and see him," she said. "Mma Makutsi will come with me, and we will have a word with Mr. Radiphuti. We will ask him whether he would like to accept my invitation, and if he says yes—and I'm sure he will—then we shall bring him straight back. That aunt of his is no problem, Mma. She is no problem at all." She paused. "And you come too, Mma Ramotswe. We shall all go."

Mma Ramotswe glanced at Mma Makutsi, and knew that she had to go. And she wanted to, anyway, as she could hardly miss the spectacle of Mma Potokwane, one of the most formidable women in Botswana, coming face-to-face with one of the country's nastiest senior aunts. It would be an encounter to remember, and talk about, for a long time. And she was sure who would win.

"You are very kind," she said to Mma Potokwane. "This will make Mma Makutsi happy, and it will be best for Phuti. It is a very good idea, Mma, and we are all grateful to you."

"I am not being kind," said Mma Potokwane. "I am just helping my friends who have helped me. Mr. J.L.B. Matekoni has done so much for us—he has fixed so many things over the years—that I am very happy to be able to repay the . . . the assistant to his wife."

That was only partly true, thought Mma Ramotswe. It was probably the case that Mma Potokwane wanted to repay favours, but it was not true that she was not kind. Of course Mma Potokwane was kind—one only had to look at her life to see that. And what was also true, Mma Ramotswe thought, was this: Some kind people may not look kind. They may look severe, or strict, or even bossy, as Mma Potokwane sometimes did. But inside them there was a big dam of kindness, as there is inside so many people, like the great dam to the south of Gaborone, ready to release its healing waters.

MMA POTOKWANE drove them to the aunt's house, parking directly outside her gate. The unpleasant brown car, with its small, mean-spirited windows, was there in the short driveway, and the aunt's front door was slightly open. A man with a rake was standing in the yard, battered old hat perched on his head; a jobbing gardener, thought Mma Ramotswe. The man waved, and she returned his wave as they approached the house.

"She is not a nice woman," muttered Mma Makutsi. "I am worried."

"Nonsense!" said Mma Potokwane, not bothering to lower her voice. "She is a melon. That is all."

They reached the front door and Mma Potokwane shouted out, *"Ko! Ko!"* When there was no reply, she shouted the greeting out again, and this time edged the front door a bit further open. This brought a reaction from within—the aunt suddenly appeared. She was wearing a pink housecoat and had a cloth, a *doek,* wound round the top of her head. She eyed her visitors suspiciously, an expression of outrage spreading slowly across her face.

"Yes?" she said. "What is this?"

"I am Mma Potokwane," came the announcement. "You know these ladies. We are here to see Mr. Radiphuti."

"Impossible," said the aunt. "He is sleeping. You must go away. All of you."

Mma Potokwane seemed to inflate before their eyes. "I am not asking you, Mma," she said to the aunt. "I am telling you. Mma Makutsi is here to see her husband."

The aunt glared at Mma Makutsi. "She is not his wife. He is not her husband. She is . . . she is *nothing,* Mma. So you must all go now. You. The nothing. This other woman. All go."

Mma Potokwane moved forward slowly. It was not really like a person moving, thought Mma Ramotswe; it was more a geological movement, the movement of boulders falling slowly down a slope—unstoppable, remorseless, obeying only the rules of gravity and no other. In the face of this, the aunt could do nothing; there was no physical contact, and Mma Potokwane moved past her into the house unimpeded. Unerringly, as if on entirely familiar territory, she made her way into a corridor, followed by Mma Makutsi and Mma Ramotswe. The first door she pushed open led into a pantry, the second into a bedroom. And there, sitting in a wheelchair by the end of the bed, was Phuti Radiphuti.

He looked up. For a few seconds his expression was one of puzzlement, but this was quickly replaced by something that Mma Ramotswe recognised as unambiguous joy. He held out a hand to Mma Makutsi, who took it and then leaned forward to embrace him.

"You have come to see me," he said. "This is very good."

"I tried to come before," she said.

"But your aunt would not allow it," said Mma Potokwane.

"And so we have come to ask you whether you would like to be looked after by me and Mma Makutsi, out at my place."

At first, Phuti seemed confused, and transferred his gaze from Mma Makutsi to Mma Ramotswe and then back again. But then he looked directly at Mma Potokwane and said, "I should like that very much, Mma. It is a very good idea." He hesitated, and then added, "When? Tomorrow?"

Mma Potokwane looked around the room in a businesslike manner. "Today," she said. "You do not seem to have many things here, Rra. But I see you have a bag, and we can put your clothes in that. And those medicines on the table—we must not forget those."

"My aunt . . . ," Phuti began.

Mma Ramotswe could see doubt creeping up on him, and she decided to speak quickly. "Mma Potokwane will talk to her again," she said. "You do not need to worry about your aunt."

The packing was completed within a few minutes. Then, with Mma Potokwane in the lead and Phuti's wheelchair being pushed by Mma Makutsi, they filed out of the room and began to make their way out of the house. They encountered the aunt near the front door, but she shrank back at the sight of Mma Potokwane, who halted for a moment and stared at her, as an elephant will face an adversary, sniffing at the wind. Indeed, Mma Ramotswe thought that she saw Mma Potokwane's ears flapping out, as an elephant's will as it prepares to charge, or feints, but she knew at once that this must be a trick of the eye, a conceit of the imagination.

The aunt said nothing, but as she went past her on the way through the door, when Mma Potokwane, Mma Makutsi, and Phuti were already outside, Mma Ramotswe stopped and spoke to her. "Listen to me, Mma," she said. "Your nephew still loves you. If you do not wish to lose him forever, then you must listen to what I say and you must remember it. Love without freedom is like a fire without air. A fire without air goes out. Do you understand me, Mma?"

She was not sure if the aunt did understand. The other woman looked up, but then looked away again. She understood, perhaps, but did not understand. There were many people like that. They understood but did not understand, all at the same time. It was a big problem.

MMA MAKUTSI helped Phuti Radiphuti settle into the room behind Mma Potokwane's office. Alone at last, he held her hand and they sat together, at first saying nothing, and then, in a rush, saying everything.

"I have cried so much," said Mma Makutsi. "I have thought of you all the time, Phuti, all the time."

He squeezed her hand. "I thought I was going to die. And when I was lying there, thinking this is the end for Radiphuti, I was only sad for you, Grace, not for me. I did not care about dying, but I did care about leaving you."

She tried to reply to this, but she could not. She found herself weeping. She took off her glasses and polished them, which is what she did at moments of emotion. Phuti took them from her, gently, and rubbed them against the sleeve of his shirt before handing them back to her.

"Mma Radiphuti," he said. "That is what you will be, very soon now."

"Very soon," she echoed. "That will be very good."

WHILE MMA MAKUTSI and Phuti Radiphuti were talking together at last, Mma Ramotswe and the matron sat together in the office itself, a freshly poured cup of tea to hand. Each also had a slice of Mma Potokwane's fruit cake on a plate beside them. There was more cake in a tin on the table, ready to be consumed if the need arose, and it surely would.

"Mr. Radiphuti seems very content," said Mma Potokwane. "Poor man."

Mma Ramotswe took a sip of her tea. "Yes. And he told me in the car that he will shortly be able to walk on a new leg they are making for him. Or part of a leg, I should say. He only needs something the length of this pencil. They did not take much off."

"We had a child with something like that," said Mma Potokwane. "He learned to walk very quickly, and ended up playing football. He had the right approach to life, that boy."

Mma Ramotswe thought about this. Having the right approach to life was a great gift in this life. Her father, the late Obed Ramotswe, had always had the right approach to life—she was sure of that. And for a moment, as she sat there with her friend, with the late-afternoon sun slanting in through the window, she thought about how she owed her father so much. He had taught her almost everything she knew about how to lead a good life, and the lessons she had learned from him were as fresh today as they ever had been. Do not complain about your life. Do not blame others for things that you have brought upon yourself. Be content with who you are and where you are, and do whatever you can do to bring to others such contentment, and joy, and understanding that you have managed to find yourself.

She closed her eyes. You can do that in the company of an old friend—you can close your eyes and think of the land that gave you life and breath, and of all the reasons why you are glad that you are there, with the people you know, with the people you love.

ABOUT THE AUTHOR

Alexander McCall Smith is also the author of the Isabel Dalhousie series, the Portuguese Irregular Verbs series, and the 44 Scotland Street series. He is professor emeritus of medical law at the University of Edinburgh and has served on many national and international bodies concerned with bioethics. He was born in what is now known as Zimbabwe and taught law at the University of Botswana. He lives in Scotland.